P9-CBY-248

HIGH-CALIBER HOLIDAY

SUSAN SLEEMAN

 HARLEQUIN® LOVE INSPIRED® SUSPENSE

Recycling programs
for this product may
not exist in your area.

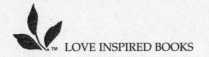 ™ LOVE INSPIRED BOOKS

ISBN-13: 978-0-373-67715-3

High-Caliber Holiday

www.Harlequin.com

Printed in U.S.A.

A scream pierced the air. Shattering glass followed.

The kitchen. Morgan.

Adrenaline rekindled in his veins. His hand on his sidearm, he closed the distance to the kitchen in a few strides. He stepped inside, his boots grinding over broken glass. Morgan stood by the sink, physically unharmed, but her face was white.

"Someone was here. He left—" Her words were barely more than a whisper.

Brady looked around. He saw nothing odd other than the glass she'd dropped on the wood floor. "Left what?"

"Those." She pointed at the countertop. "I didn't leave them there."

Brady looked at the counter, then back at her ashen face. His pulse kicked into high gear, and he drew his weapon. It was a good thing he'd walked Morgan home. A very good thing.

Brady needed to check the other rooms for an intruder, but he also wanted to take a better look at the photograph lying under a long-stemmed red rose.

The downright creepy photo was an engagement announcement. A man sat next to Morgan, but some picture-editing program had left only a silhouette with the words *Your One True Love* superimposed on it. The caption below read, "You are mine. You will marry no one but me."

Susan Sleeman is a bestselling author of inspirational and clean-read romantic suspense books and mysteries. Awards include RT Reviewers' Choice Best Book for *Thread of Suspicion*; *No Way Out* and *The Christmas Witness* were finalists for the Daphne du Maurier Award for Excellence. She's had the pleasure of living in nine states and currently lives in Oregon. To learn more about Susan visit her website at susansleeman.com.

Books by Susan Sleeman

Love Inspired Suspense

First Responders

Silent Night Standoff
Explosive Alliance
High-Caliber Holiday

The Justice Agency

Double Exposure
Dead Wrong
No Way Out
Thread of Suspicion
Dark Tide

High-Stakes Inheritance
Behind the Badge
The Christmas Witness
Holiday Defenders
"Special Ops Christmas"

Visit the Author Profile page at Harlequin.com for more titles.

And my God will meet all your needs according to the riches of his glory in Christ Jesus.
–Philippians 4:19

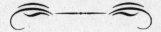

For the many law enforcement and military snipers who perform such a necessary job to keep all of us safe. Thank you for your service even when people often don't understand and appreciate the job you do.

ONE

The gun couldn't be real. Could it?

Morgan Thorsby clutched her friend Lacy's arm and scooted back from the gun-wielding man charging onto the MAX light rail train. Brisk, chilling air rushed in behind him as she looked at the silvery gun glinting in the overhead light.

The weapon looked real. Very real.

The man took a step closer. Anger radiated from his body. His breathing was ragged as he made a quick survey of the space, skimming tortured eyes over the few passengers on board this late at night.

Please, God, don't let this be real, Morgan begged, her heart thumping in her chest. She fought to control her fear and studied the man's jittery behavior.

Could he be one of those shooters who'd been pushed beyond his breaking point until he'd decided to randomly kill people? She couldn't just sit here and wait to find out. Her life was in immediate danger and it was up to her to protect herself. She had to do something, but what?

Run. Hide. Fight. The active shooter video she'd viewed at work rushed through her mind. The video taught them not to sit back passively but to run, hide or fight. She couldn't run. She couldn't hide. She could fight. But how? With what?

She searched the train looking for a weapon. Any weapon.

The man's distressed gaze landed on her with a finality that took her breath away.

"He's coming toward us." Lacy grabbed Morgan's hand.

"Don't panic," Morgan said and forced herself to look into the gunman's eyes. She saw no life in the depths. Desperation, panic, yes, but nothing to prove he was alive.

Oh no. No.

She knew this man. She'd seen him in the sea of men and women who'd brought a class-action lawsuit against her family's company, claiming Thorsby Mill had polluted the water and caused cancer in the residents. As the company's attorney at that time, she'd seen the plaintiffs' turmoil day in and day out during the trial.

Plaintiffs who'd threatened her life then and continued to send threatening letters after the mill had been cleared of any wrongdoing. The gunman was one of those people. And that meant he'd come for her. Her alone.

Her heart raced faster. Beating at an unstoppable gallop.

He continued moving, his ragged jeans whispering through the quiet. Step by step, he advanced on her, purpose in each thump of his dirty boots on the metal floor. Hatred spewed from his expression.

Morgan felt time stop. She was aware of Lacy's touch. Of the cold. The icy cold. Her palms starting to sweat. The bag holding a Christmas present for her mother slid from her fingers, the crystal vase falling to the floor. The sound of breaking glass caught his attention, distracting him for a moment. But it all seemed to be happening at the end of a tunnel. In a foggy haze. All except the gun. It was clear and sharp and she could reach out to touch it.

Lacy clutched Morgan's hand tighter, drawing her attention. Lacy didn't deserve to be a party to this. Morgan had to do everything she could to portray strength and confidence for her friend, to ease her fear. Morgan sat up straighter. Firmed her shoulders. Jutted out her jaw and waited for him to act.

Eyes riveted to her, he took the last few steps. He raised the gun. Slowly. Purposefully. He planted it on her temple. The cool steel bit into her skin, and she recoiled in fear.

"Don't back away, Morgan," he said, his voice flat, as if he took hostages every day.

She could smell the sour stench of alcohol radiating from him. The blood drained from her head. She felt weak. Powerless.

"I've come for you. To pay you back. Just like I promised I would in my letter." He glared down on her. "Your stinkin' mill has taken my entire family, and it's time for you to pay."

Anything she said would make him angrier so she didn't speak at all, but waited for his finger to drift to the trigger.

Silence descended on them, coursing through the space, tight, pervasive, building into a frenzy. A pressure cooker ready to erupt.

An announcement carried into the silence, warning that the doors would soon close. His eyes grew wilder, his hold on reality a mere thread. Seconds ticked by, feeling like an hour. Panic threatened to swamp her.

A twisted, mean smile claimed his thin lips as the doors whooshed together, cocooning her inside the car with a killer. The train set off, the side-to-side motion rocking Morgan, but the gunman stood strong, his weapon never wavering.

With the gun at her head, she couldn't form a coherent thought except that she was going to die. She didn't know what he was waiting for, but he simply stood there. Watching. Maybe enjoying her terror. Wanting to make her suffer as his family suffered.

Focus. Now. Figure a way out of this.

The train slowed for the next stop, brakes squealing as they bit into the metal. Doors slid open. A rush of freezing air sliced into the train. There were no passengers waiting on the platform to board. The only other passenger on the train, a man in the back of the car, bolted out the door. Quick, staccato steps took him outside and into the cover of darkness.

The gunman didn't turn. Didn't see. Didn't notice.

Lacy. Morgan could save Lacy the same way.

Morgan forced herself to make eye contact with him. "You're not upset with my friend. Just me. Can she please get off?"

He eyed Lacy for a moment. She cringed. He took a breath and gave the briefest of nods. "Go now. Before I change my mind."

She stood slowly and looked back at Morgan, regret hanging in her eyes.

"Go," Morgan said. "I'll be fine."

"Ha!" he shouted, sending Lacy fleeing. "You'll be as fine as all of my family and friends your greedy family killed."

Morgan ignored his words and kept watch on Lacy as she scurried through the falling snow into the dark shadows of the buildings. Good. She was safe. The car was now empty. If he fired his weapon, she'd be the only one injured.

The doors slid on the track, closing with a thump of finality.

"Now we're alone, and we can get down to business," he said.

Business. Meaning her death.

Time slowed and she was aware of everything around her. The grating of the train as they took a curve. The pungent scent of his alcohol. The unmistakable cloying smell of fear in the air.

"Do you even know who I am?" he sneered.

Morgan wished she could say she knew his name, but the plaintiff list was long and she couldn't identify them all. She knew the truth was plastered on her face so she didn't speak a word.

"You don't know me, do you?" He shifted and pressed the gun deeper into her forehead. "I'm not surprised. Not after your coldhearted representation in the trial."

He huffed out a laugh and ground the gun into her skin, his eyes fixed on hers. "Well, know this, Morgan Thorsby. I'm Craig Shaw and everyone will soon know my name. The minute we reach the last stop, I'm the man who's going to drag you off this train, haul you out to your precious mill and end your life."

Brady Owens listened to the hum of tires as the First Response Squad raced toward MAX's final Yellow Line stop near Portland State University. A 911 call from the train operator who'd been listening into the hostage situation told them the shooter planned to disembark with his hostage at this stop.

"ETA two minutes," team leader Jake Marsh announced from the driver's seat.

"Roger that," Brady said, his pulse ratcheting up at the call to action.

His fellow FRS members sitting on bench seats in the rear of the truck responded with somber affirmatives. Negotiator Archer Reed bowed his head in prayer. He would carry the heaviest duty tonight, talking the gunman down, hopefully preventing the need for Brady's services as the team sniper. Paramedic Darcie Stevens would render aid to the traumatized woman and anyone injured in the incident. Jake would direct the action and bomb tech Cash Dixon would fill in wherever Jake asked. The only one missing from their six-person emergency response team was their other negotiator, Skyler, who was on her honeymoon.

Brady couldn't imagine any other people he'd want to take with him into the tense situation awaiting them. All team members except Darcie were sworn sheriff's deputies who fulfilled other job responsibilities when they weren't responding to an emergency. Though assigned to the county sheriff's department, they were dispatched to handle negotiations and major emergencies for the entire Portland metro area regardless of county lines.

"We're here." Jake swung their mobile command center the size of a package delivery truck to the curb out of view of the MAX stop.

Even late at night, students would be milling about. The team would contain the shooter in the train and cordon off the area to protect innocent lives. Then Archer would use the train's PA system to communicate with the gunman.

That was the plan. But they had no time to run the scenario, and plans could go wrong.

Curling his .330 Winchester Magnum rifle closer, Brady mentally checked off his steps. Ammo first. Check. Already loaded in his rifle. If he had to shoot, it would be through glass, requiring special ammo to reduce deflection on glass penetration. Extra ammo was in his vest. Scope was fixed and calibrated. Binoculars and laser range finder snug in his pocket. He patted his vest pocket to confirm. He was ready. He could do this.

Jake cut the engine, then joined the team. He glanced at Darryl Collins, the computer tech assigned to their team, who sat behind a console. "We have eyes or ears on the train yet?"

"I'm still working with the MAX tech team to patch us through."

"Well, get 'em. No way we're going in blind." Jake eyed the team, his gaze sharp and focused. "The gunman is not getting off the train with Morgan Thorsby and she's getting out of this alive and well. You got that?"

They nodded.

"You have your assignments." Jake clapped his hands. "Let's roll."

Brady slung his rifle over his shoulder and headed into the night, toward the perfect location he'd chosen in a yard abutting an apartment complex. He jogged across the road and slipped through the gate. Resting his arm on a fence post topped with snow, he took a shooting stance. He'd like to get into a more natural position, but that wasn't an option. No problem. He'd made shots in every position imaginable as a Marine Scout Sniper. He sighted in the scope and adjusted for the wind.

"Falcon, in position," he said into his microphone.

"Roger that, Falcon," came Jake's response. "Stand by. Train ETA in one minute. Audio streaming."

With more than one agency responding to the incident, they would use code names when communicating. The group had long ago voted on an animal name for each person. Brady was tagged Falcon, as the bird and he both moved fast. Cash got Termite since they were demolitions experts. Archer, Mockingbird for his soothing voice. And Jake? He had the best name of all. Papa Bear.

"Got eyes and ears, sir," Darryl's voice came over Brady's earpiece.

"Then we're a go, Falcon," Jake said. "TriMet has confirmed the doors will remain closed on this car and Mockingbird is patched through to the train. We'll give Termite time to escort passengers in the other cars to a secured spot, then Mockingbird will take over."

"Roger that, Papa Bear," Brady confirmed. "I'm ready."

But was he ready? He wasn't sure. Not completely, anyway. Not after their last callout, when he'd hesitated to take the shot. He was good with taking extreme measures for hostage-taking criminals and drug dealers, but the prior callout involved a former marine. Brady had felt like he was taking out a family member. Couldn't be helped, though. The man had lost touch with reality. If Brady hadn't acted, the guy would have killed his wife and three sweet children.

Now Brady wasn't sure how he'd react when it came time to pull the trigger.

The train rolled in, the brakes squealing to a stop.

Focus, man. Focus. He fine-tuned his scope and shut out everything around him. The biting wind. The falling snow. The flag flapping on the next building. The sound of Cash moving people out of the line of fire. All of it faded into the background, his eye fixed dead center on his scope.

The occupants of the car came into focus in the crosshairs. Morgan Thorsby was blonde, petite and wearing a trench coat tied over what looked like an expensive suit, but it was the gunman, Craig Shaw, who Brady was most interested in.

Brady adjusted his scope. Sighted on the T-zone of Craig's head.

"I have a target, but no shot. No shot." Brady kept his eyes on the scope, but wouldn't shoot before an attempt was made to end this standoff without loss of life.

"Craig," Archer's voice came over the train's speaker.

Craig's head shot up. "Who's that? How do you know me?"

Brady listened through his earpiece as Archer introduced himself and started the process of talking Craig into surrendering.

Craig seemed to listen, then suddenly pivoted and pounded on the door, the sound reverberating through the silent car. "Open it now or I'll kill Morgan right here!"

"Don't do anything rash, Craig," Archer said over the train's speaker. "We've got all the time in the world to talk this through."

"I don't want to talk," Craig screamed. "I want out of this tin can, now!"

"I'm afraid I don't have the ability to open the doors, Craig." Archer was a tough law enforcement officer. Sharp. Intense, but he also had a soothing way about him and his voice was unhurried and comforting.

"I don't care, man," Craig fired back. "Get

these doors open or I will shoot her. I swear I will. You've got five minutes. You hear me? Five minutes. If I'm still locked in here then, she dies."

TWO

"Dumb cops," Craig muttered as he gestured at the door with his gun. He obviously thought Archer was no longer listening, but Brady knew his teammate was not only listening, he was intently watching.

"I could help you with them," Morgan Thorsby said. "As an attorney, I can act as a go-between to negotiate your demands."

"Demands? I don't have demands. I just want to get off the stupid train with you in tow." He massaged his forehead with his free hand.

"They'll let you off if you surrender your gun," Morgan continued.

Brady was surprised she had the presence of mind to talk so calmly to a man holding her life in his hands. Even more surprising, Archer didn't shut her down. Maybe she was saying the right things and Archer thought she could help.

"And then what?" Craig asked. "I step off the train and some hotshot kills me? No, thanks."

"You have it backwards. If you don't surrender the gun, that hotshot you mentioned is going to go to work and you won't get off the train alive."

"Fine. But if that happens, I'm taking you with me." He grabbed Morgan and jerked her head back, planting the gun against her temple again.

"Wait. Let me talk to the negotiator when he comes back on. I'll tell him you haven't harmed anyone and that you're going to surrender. You can give me the gun, and we can walk out together. Then I'll represent you or find a good criminal lawyer for you."

Brady heard the underlying tremble in Morgan's tone but it was still soothing, almost hypnotic. If Brady were the shooter, he would gladly do what she asked.

Craig took a step back. "You'd represent me, even after this?"

"Yes," she said. "You've been drinking to mask your loss. If you had a clear head, you—"

"I'd do the same thing."

The guy's biting tone said he was planning to pull that trigger. It made Brady want to end this now, but he wouldn't do so without Jake's authority.

Craig stood unmoving and staring at her. Suddenly, something caught his attention in the distance and he spun.

"No!" he shouted. "It's a trick. I can see them—

all of them—cops…coming for me. Well, they won't find me. I'll make my own way out."

He jerked his finger. The gun erupted. Bullets blasted into the window, the safety glass cracking and splintering, but holding.

"Falcon, you are clear to take a shot," Jake announced.

"Roger that, Papa Bear." Brady's gut cramped as he dropped his finger to the trigger. Took a deep breath. Released a long hiss of air. Prepared to squeeze. Craig—*no, the target*, Brady reminded himself—shifted, his eyes coming into view. Filled with rage, with pain.

Brady hesitated.

Craig started for Morgan, bending toward her. Brady had to act now or the window of opportunity would be gone. He quickly adjusted and squeezed the trigger. The bullet sliced through the air. Craig suddenly lurched forward, Morgan falling in the other direction. She hit the ground, disappearing from the scope.

Brady's mouth dropped open. He didn't think his shot hit Craig. Looked more like he'd fallen. But what about Morgan? His bullet couldn't have hit her, could it? Even if it hadn't, his moment of hesitation had given Craig a chance to move closer to Morgan and changed Brady's angle. Maybe it had put Morgan in the path of shattering glass. He wouldn't know until he had a chance to get inside the train car and look around.

"Move, move, move," came Jake's voice as he dispatched the team to secure the gunman and train.

Brady kept his scope honed on the train when all he wanted to do was race across the street and see if Morgan was alive. He couldn't, though. He had to hold his position until Jake gave the all clear.

He waited. Watched.

The team charged the train. The doors slid open. Brady caught a look at Craig and Morgan on the floor. Blood colored Morgan's arm. *Good.* If Brady had hit her, it wasn't a body shot. She should make it.

She held up Craig's gun. Looked like it hadn't been her injury taking her down. Instead, she'd dropped to the floor to retrieve the gun. Archer put a knee in Craig's back and cuffed him. Jake retrieved Craig's gun while Cash went to Morgan and comforted her.

"Stand down, Falcon," Jake said.

Brady wasted no time strapping his rifle over his shoulder and taking off toward the train, moving as fast as he could. His gaze went straight to Morgan. On the floor, sitting up and alert, she'd clamped a hand over her injured arm. Blood had oozed through her fingers. Fresh. Red. But no longer increasing.

Brady sighed out his relief. Guilt flooded in. His hesitation had likely caused her injury. Still, it could have been far worse. He could have severely injured her.

Thank You, God, for protecting her, he thought and joined Cash who was standing over her and calling on his radio for Darcie.

"Hang tight," Cash said to Morgan. "Our medic is on the way."

"Seems like the bleeding has stopped," Morgan said, not sounding as fearful as Brady expected.

Sure, lingering fear darkened her eyes, but he liked the strength he saw in her. She was something else. Most women would be fainting or falling apart in this situation, but Morgan remained strong.

Brady's kind of woman. Not clingy. Not needy. Her own person, standing strong. Until he shot her. Or his bullet sent glass flying into her arm.

Right. She's hurt because of me. He should apologize for the injury, but to do so, he'd have to admit he'd frozen, and his hesitation could very well have caused her injury.

He'd have to find a way to deal with that. Because one thing he knew for certain, a sniper who froze wasn't good for anyone, least of all the First Response Squad. The only way to combat that was to get over what was causing it or leave the team.

Icy-cold air laden with flurrying snow rushed into the train car as Morgan reached for a pole to get to her feet. It hit her then. She'd been shot. Shot! It was only a superficial wound, but even so, a bullet had grazed her arm.

A bullet. An honest-to-goodness bullet.

The night came flashing back like a fast-forwarded video. The pictures were bright, but blurred. The sounds frantic. Craig coming for her, wanting to kill her, his bullets piercing the glass, sending spidery cracks racing through it. Her decision to put the active shooter training into practice. To fight. When Craig no longer had his gun planted against her head, she'd shot out her foot and tripped him. It was risky, but she'd had no choice. He was going to kill her. Right there in the train if she did nothing.

He'd crashed to the floor. The gun skittered away. She'd started to go after it when another gun blast sounded from a distance. The zip of a bullet was followed by the slice in her arm, pain radiating up. But she'd kept her cool and located the gun before Craig could get to his feet.

She shuddered and forced her thoughts to the present. The deputy who'd called for a medic was hauling Craig off in handcuffs. His face was peppered with cuts from the glass. His shoulder was bloody, but he didn't seem to notice.

He came to a stop next to Morgan and glared at her. "Don't think this is the last of this. I'll make you pay."

"Pretty hard to do from prison," the deputy said.

Craig sneered at her. "I'll find a way."

"Come on, Shaw." The deputy jerked Craig's cuffs and prodded him off the train.

With Craig gone, she was suddenly aware of another deputy who'd arrived later than the others staring down at her. He stood tall and commanding as if protecting her from an unseen foe.

Unseen foe. Ha! A thought she'd never expected to have.

It was all so surreal, and she couldn't handle much more. She needed to give her statement and get out of there before she fell apart. First, she had to get off the floor, out of the glass and away from the blood.

She pulled up on the pole. Her knees buckled and the blood drained from her head. She wobbled.

"Are you okay, ma'am?" the deputy asked. The car seemed to be spinning, and it was all she could do to find a seat before hitting the floor.

"Head between your knees or you're going to keel over." He stepped forward and a strong hand pushed her head down, then held it in place.

A whooshing noise rushed through Morgan's ears, and she blinked hard to try to clear the dizziness. She was aware of movement around her and the man's foot as he tapped on the metal floor, as if anxious to leave. Her vision was starting to clear, and she tried to sit up.

"Not yet," he said, obviously used to getting his way.

She waited a few more moments. "I'm good to sit up."

"You're sure you won't faint on me?" His tone had lightened. "'Cause superhero code says a damsel in distress can only be rescued once a day." He grinned.

"No worries. I don't need rescuing, by you or anyone else," she replied more vehemently than called for. He was simply trying to alleviate her stress with a joke, but she was tired of people thinking she needed taking care of.

"Have it your way." His hand retracted.

She shot up. Her head spun. She closed her eyes and waited it out.

"Maybe you should've taken your time sitting up there," he said, a Midwestern flavor to his tone.

She opened her eyes and glared up at him. Her gaze had to travel quite a distance to reach his eyes. Past a broad chest. Past some very nice shoulders, to a handsome face. With his blond hair worn in a messy style, he looked more like a laid-back surfer than a cop.

How in the world had she missed him when he'd come barreling into the car? Sure, all the deputies were fine-looking men, but something about this one made her want to linger on his flinty-black eyes that watched her intently as she studied him.

"Deputy Brady Owens at your service," he said as his lips turned up in a dazzling smile that she assumed made women swoon, but she could see it was forced. His eyes were troubled. He wore the same uniform as the others, black tactical pants and a polo shirt with a Kevlar vest on top, but an expensive-looking rifle with a high-powered scope hung over his shoulder. He didn't at all seem the type to carry a rifle.

Rifle? Wait.

"You're the sniper," she said, her mind processing the fact that this man standing here ended lives with a simple pull of the trigger.

He gave a clipped nod but said nothing else, leaving her feeling uneasy.

"How does someone get a job like that? I mean, do you wake up one morning and say I think I'll learn how to shoot people?" She knew she was rambling and sounding rude, but she'd never met anyone with this job and didn't know what to say to him.

"Marines needed me, ma'am, and I did my duty." He stood taller and gone was the easygoing expression. It was now stony and unyielding. "Our armed forces are the reason you have the freedom to offer representation to a man who takes a woman hostage at gunpoint. And the reason that police officers can save lives in hostage situations like this one."

"Wait," she said quickly. "No…I'm sorry. I

didn't mean anything by my comment. I was just wondering about it, that's all. I meant no disrespect. I appreciate the men and women of the military and the police."

He looked doubtful before his gaze lifted above her. She swiveled to see what he was looking at.

A woman wearing the same black uniform and a stethoscope hanging around her neck marched forward. The thirty-something woman looked familiar, but Morgan wasn't sure from where. When she got closer, their eyes connected.

The woman smiled. "Hi, Morgan. It's me, Darcie. Remember? From OSU."

Morgan rose slowly, searching her memory for a Darcie and testing her strength before stepping toward the door. As she got closer, the picture of a young girl in her philosophy class as naive as Morgan had been swirled in Morgan's mind. "Darcie Wiggins?"

She nodded. "Not Wiggins anymore, but Stevens, and yeah, it's me."

"Of course," Morgan said. "I'm surprised you remember me."

"I'd never forget the girl who set off to save the world one person at a time."

"Oh, *that* girl. She's long gone." Morgan laughed and grabbed her old Oregon State University friend in a hug, but pulled back when the pain in her arm made her wince. "Crazy to run into you here. I thought you were working as an

ER nurse. What happened? Did the ER get too tame for you and you had to move on to the front lines?"

"Changed jobs a few years back," Darcie said, her impenetrable tone stopping Morgan from asking additional questions.

"Ms. Thorsby just about passed out," Brady inserted. "She put her head between her knees for a bit and seems better. She either took a bullet or got in the way of flying glass, but the bleeding's stopped." He frowned as if the situation bothered him personally. This man, the one whose bullet cut like butter through the glass and whizzed by her, was concerned for her?

An uncontrollable tremble started at her head and rushed down her body. "It was a bullet. At least it felt like one."

His frown deepened.

"Go ahead and sit down, Morgan, and I'll take a look at it." Darcie dropped onto the chair next to Morgan and started poking at the wound. "Superficial. Not from glass. Odd," she said, and paused to look up at Brady. "The wound is thicker than I'd expect from the rounds Shaw was firing."

"Meaning what?" Morgan asked as she swung her gaze between the two of them.

Darcie smiled at Morgan, but it was forced. "It should heal quickly, but it's gonna hurt like crazy for some time."

She didn't have to tell Morgan that. As the

adrenaline ebbed, the pain became more acute. Or maybe the flashes of her near death were making her more aware of everything around her.

Darcie moved on to Morgan's vitals and strapped a blood pressure cuff on her arm. Brady continued to stand beside them, his arms raised, his hands clinging to an overhead bar. Tapping a finger on the metal, he stared down on Morgan, making her aware of his every movement. Aware of his muscles flexing as he moved, which he did. A lot.

"I heard the whole conversation with Craig." Darcie removed the cuff. "Did I hear you right? You're not representing Thorsby Mill anymore?"

The last thing Morgan wanted to talk about was the lawsuit, but she didn't want to be rude and it would take her mind off the man hovering over her. Maybe keep thoughts of Craig at bay, too. "I changed jobs a few months ago."

"Are you with a local firm?" Darcie dug bandages and antiseptic from her bag.

Morgan shook her head. "I'm not practicing law at all. I'm directing a local jobs program. Portland Employment Assistance—PEA for short. We help unemployed people seeking government assistance to find jobs."

That brought a look of surprise to Brady's face, and Morgan was starting to wonder why she was noticing every little thing he did.

Darcie's hand stilled midair. "Wow, I never imagined you'd leave the law."

Morgan shrugged. "We had this particularly contentious class action lawsuit that consumed my life for the last few years. Burned me out and I just couldn't do it anymore."

"Class action, huh? That's what the shooter was talking about. But what happened? I mean a lawsuit against a paper mill seems odd." Darcie went back to her bag.

"Surprising, right?" Morgan dug deep for the will to discuss something she never wanted to think about again.

"It's okay if you don't want to talk about it," Darcie said. "I understand."

Morgan drew an uneasy breath. "A couple of years ago people downriver from the plant started getting cancer in record numbers. They claimed we dumped chemicals in the river, causing the cancer. Of course, that didn't happen and water tests proved our story, but it still wasn't easy to defend against."

Darcie applied antiseptic to Morgan's wound, the sharp sting taking all of her concentration. She bit her tongue to keep from crying out and seeming weak.

"People sue at the drop of a hat these days," Darcie said.

"Honestly, I could hardly blame them," Morgan rushed on, trying to ignore the pain. "A larger than normal distribution of a single type of cancer in their small population was unusual. They wanted to blame someone. And find money to cover medical bills."

Darcie looked up. "You won, though, right? And that's why this Craig guy was so angry?"

Morgan nodded but an uncontrolled sigh slipped out over the memory of the mental and physical cost that winning had taken on her life. She had to change the subject before Darcie pried any deeper. "And you... Stevens, now. You're married."

"Was. Not anymore." Darcie applied the bandage.

"You two gonna gab all night or can we get moving?" Brady's voice broke in.

Darcie offered him a thankful smile. She seemed glad he'd jumped in. Was she not willing to share about her past? It made Morgan even more curious about her old friend.

"We should get together for lunch and catch up." Morgan looked up at Brady. "When we don't have an armed deputy standing over us."

"Who, Brady?" Darcie chuckled as she secured the gauze bandage. "He's so laid-back, I sometimes forget that he's this intense sniper guy."

"Come on, Darcie." He mocked a knife to the chest and grinned. "Don't hurt my cred like this."

He fixed a genuine, easygoing smile on Morgan, softening the hard, angular lines of his face. Making him even more handsome and difficult to look away from. She shouldn't be noticing. Should be looking anywhere except at him, but he was like a puzzle waiting to be solved.

One minute he was easygoing, the next intense and fierce. Both attractive. Both needed to be avoided. If she was going to get her life back on firm footing after her recent move and job change, she had no time for romance.

"So," she said to Darcie. "Am I cleared to go?"

Darcie sat back and started packing up her case. "My official response is that you should have your arm checked out at the hospital."

"And unofficially?"

"Put some antibiotic cream on the wound. Keep it bandaged and change it once a day. If it doesn't heal or becomes red, puffy or painful see a doctor."

"I'll take the unofficial advice so I can get out of here."

"Sorry, friend." Darcie squeezed Morgan's knee. "You'll have to stay to give your statement and answer questions. Brady will escort you back to the command post."

"She's right," he said coming to full attention. "The detectives will want to talk to you."

Right. She'd have to relive the experience, play by play, all over again.

She supposed it would be better to do so here with people surrounding her than at home alone.

That would come later, she knew. Much later. When she had nothing to distract her.

No handsome guy. No old friend. No pretense of a smile. Not even the shock, which would have worn off by then.

She'd be alone in her new apartment. In the dark. Recounting each terrifying second of the ordeal and trying hard to remember why she'd so desperately wanted to stand on her own two feet.

THREE

Wind whistled through the FRS truck, but at least the snow had let up. Brady wanted to head home, sit in front of a roaring fire and have time alone to process the night. He'd pull out the small chunks of wood he'd cut to carve into ornaments for the FRS team and whittle long strips into the flames. But first, he had to help the team button down the specialty truck. Then they would meet to debrief and wind down in the communal living space of a remodeled historic firehouse where they all lived in private condos on the upper floors.

Brady was required to attend the debrief, but then he'd go straight to his condo. After a shooting, even one that hadn't ended in the loss of a life, he liked to decompress on his own. The sooner the better. And that meant getting the truck loaded so they could all get home.

He stowed his rifle case in a bench seat midway in the truck and turned to find Darcie watching him. He suspected she wanted to ask about the graze on Morgan's arm. Darcie couldn't prove the injury had come from Brady's rifle, no one could, but the thickness of the wound was a good indicator that he'd been the one to shoot Morgan.

"What?" he asked, when he couldn't stand her eyes on him any longer.

She continued to watch him as a mother might watch a wayward child. "I have a favor to ask."

He wasn't in any frame of mind to do her favor, but he would hear her out. "Okay."

"Can you hang around and escort Morgan home? She lives a few blocks away, and I don't want her walking home alone after this."

He let out a breath and almost offered a quick yes. After all, Morgan was a real beauty. And tough. But there was also something vulnerable about her. He'd seen it when he'd left her with the detectives. Like she needed him. Not just now, but long term.

Too bad. He wasn't in a position to be needed by any woman. And especially not a woman who was all wrong for him. She was a lawyer, for Pete's sake. Dressed in an expensive coat and suit. Shoes and purse that screamed *designer*. A last name that everyone in town knew from her father's involvement in the business world.

No, a guy from the wrong side of the tracks didn't need the heartache that would come with such a relationship.

He closed the bench and looked at Darcie. "I'm sure the detectives will give her a ride."

"You're right. They will, especially if there might be someone else out to get her." Darcie shivered.

"The detectives can protect her."

"I know that, too, but I'm concerned for more than her physical safety. She and I go way back, and I want to make sure she's okay. You know... really okay. That she's not going to freak out when she steps inside her apartment, closes the door and thoughts of the gun-wielding creep take over—which we both know could happen. You're good at reading people. You'll be able to tell if she shouldn't be left alone."

"So are you. Why not go with her yourself?"

"A, I may carry a weapon because I'd never hear the end of it from you guys if I didn't, but I'm not skilled at protecting someone. And B, I'm on duty in an hour. You're not." She watched him carefully, her motherly concern still evident on her face. She'd lost her only child four years ago, but instead of the loss leaving her cold it had caused her to transfer her motherly devotion to the people around her—especially her team members. "You're usually one of the first guys to step up and help someone. What's different with Morgan?"

He wasn't about to admit that Morgan's vulnerability made him wary of getting too close to her. She needed someone. He got that. It just couldn't be him. Not now, when he was struggling to do his job. And not with a woman like Morgan. He'd learned his lesson in high school about mixing with a girl out of his league and wouldn't repeat that mistake.

"Okay, then. Maybe Archer can do it." Darcie started to walk away.

She only had to take two steps before he felt like a real heel. "Wait, Darcie. I'll do it."

She smiled her thanks and it wasn't hard to see she'd known he'd cave. All the guys on the team believed in defending the downtrodden, so her assumption wasn't a stretch, but it still irked him. "I'll go tell Jake."

"No need. I already told him." She smiled.

"You were that certain I'd do it, huh?"

"I'm certain that you're a good man, Brady Owens, and you'd never let a woman who'd been through a terrifying standoff walk home alone."

He wrapped Darcie under his arm and knuckled her head. "And you, my friend, are a master manipulator."

"Guilty." She grinned up at him as she freed herself. "I'll go say goodbye to Morgan and tell her you'll escort her home. Call me if she needs anything."

Brady took his time packing up his vest and helping the other team members, but soon there was nothing left to do so he climbed down from the truck. He watched the team drive off, then went to the command post.

Morgan sat in a metal folding chair, her hands clasped in her lap, her body shivering in the biting wind. Detective Rossi, a thick and pudgy man with a wild head of black hair and a dark complexion that went perfectly with the Italian name, stood over her.

He looked up when Brady approached. "Help you, deputy?"

"I'll be escorting Ms. Thorsby home."

Morgan's focus swiveled to him and she opened her mouth as if to argue, but then clamped down on her lips.

Rossi nodded. "An escort is a wise idea. She just told me she's received additional threatening letters from plaintiffs."

Brady glanced at her to see how she was doing with these ongoing threats. She was biting down on her lip even harder.

He turned back to the detective. "Are you planning to look into these threats?"

"You can be assured I'll be following up on each letter." He fixed a firm gaze on Morgan. "As I said, I'm glad Owens is escorting you home, but he won't be around to watch your back after that. You'll need to be careful until I can make sure there aren't any other crazies out there who want to attack you."

Morgan shivered again. From the cold? Maybe. Or from Rossi's dire tone? More likely.

Brady would had liked to offer Morgan encouragement here, but if what she said about the letters was true, he didn't think Rossi was overreacting. Not one bit. Brady couldn't help with her fear, but he could solve her problem with the cold. He shrugged out of his coat and settled it over her shoulders.

Her eyes flashed wide in surprise. "Thank you, but I can't take your jacket."

"You've had a much harder night than I have and you deserve to be warm."

"But I—"

Brady held up a hand stilling her and focused on Rossi. "Is Ms. Thorsby free to go?"

Rossi nodded, then handed a business card to Morgan. "Get those threats to me ASAP."

She took the card and Rossi produced another one for Brady. "Just in case you need to contact me for anything."

"You ready, Ms. Thorsby?" Brady asked.

"It's Morgan, and yes, I'm very ready." She rose, and despite his heavy coat, she trembled.

"I'm Brady, by the way, in case you didn't catch that," he said, lightening his tone to help ease her anxiety. "I'm sorry you had to go through all of this." He made sure his apology carried his sincere regret. Not only for the situation, but for her injury, as well.

"Thank you. I'm just glad it all worked out okay. If I hadn't tripped Craig at the end to send the gun flying, things might have been far different." She sighed and started toward the sidewalk.

So that's what had happened and why she'd fallen to the ground. Not that it eased Brady's conscience.

"We see vulnerable and disillusioned people all the time at PEA," she continued. "Puts us at risk for one of them going off on us, so we regularly train on active shooter scenarios." She looked up at him. "Have you seen the 'Run. Hide. Fight.' video made by Homeland Security?"

He nodded. "Our agency uses it in training all the time. Especially at schools and with people who come in contact with the public. We also suggest people watch it on YouTube." He smiled at her. "Sounds like it worked for you, reminding you to take action. If you hadn't…"

She frowned, and he decided it was best to move on to something other than tonight's incident.

"Are you from this part of town?" he asked.

She shook her head. "I've only lived in the city for a few months. I'm a suburban girl. West Linn."

He knew all about the pricey suburb. "City living must be very different for you, then."

"Exactly," she said vehemently.

He suspected there was a story there, but his

job was to walk her home, not learn all he could about her.

He picked up his pace, escorting her past looky-loos who lingered at the edge of the crime scene, probably still hoping for a shootout or other action they could film for social media. Morgan didn't seem to notice them. Brady supposed she was lost in her thoughts, likely replaying the night. Darcie had been right. Not that Brady would ever tell her that. Morgan needed someone to make sure she was okay. Whether he liked it or not, he was tasked with that duty.

"This is me." She stopped outside a historic redbrick apartment building and dug out her keys. She returned his jacket, then held out her hand. "Thanks for walking me home, Brady. It wasn't necessary, but I really do appreciate it."

He considered shaking her hand and taking off, but he'd be in a heap of trouble if he ignored Darcie's command to make sure Morgan got into her apartment all right. "I'll see you inside before I go."

She crossed her arms and eyed him, but he wouldn't let that deter him. He'd rather face her wrath than Darcie's. He started up the steps before Morgan could argue, then stood to the side while she unlocked the street entrance. They stepped inside, and as he stomped his feet to clear the snow, he admired the small but ornate lobby. A tall Christmas tree sat in the corner covered with white twinkling lights and white balls. Simple and elegant, like the costly apartment building.

Christmas, ha! The last thing he wanted to think about. Early December was way too soon to start. He'd actually prefer never to think about. Just brought back bad childhood memories. He'd only ever received one Christmas present the year his mother had managed to stay sober. Still, he couldn't ignore the holiday the way he had before joining the FRS. Skyler had decorated their firehouse in November for her annual Christmas party for homeless families. She loved the season. He didn't, but he wouldn't go all Scrooge and ruin it for her or the others on the team.

They boarded the old elevator car with wood paneling and brass furnishings.

"How old is this building?" he asked when the silence in the small space turned uncomfortable.

"It was built in 1910 and just recently restored." Morgan's eyes lit up, and he had to look away before he stared at the captivating sight she made. "I love that the renovations stayed true to the time period. I'd have hated it if they'd made the apartments sleek and modern like my parents' home."

She'd just moved to the city from West Linn. Was it possible she'd lived with her family until she'd moved here? If so, it was totally in opposition to the independence she seemed to exude, piquing his curiosity even more.

He leaned back against the wall, listening to

the elevator's ancient motor carry them to the top floor where the bell's sharp ping cut through the quiet.

"Penthouse," he said jokingly.

"Hardly." She frowned.

At her door, he reached for the keys. Their fingers touched and unexpected warmth spread through him. She hastily stepped back, nearly dropping the keys, but her eyes remained riveted to his. He could see she was interested in him.

So he wasn't the only one. Interesting.

She took another step back from him.

Even more interesting. She didn't want to feel anything for him. Slumming it with a guy like him was probably the furthest thing from her mind. Or, for all he knew, she was involved with someone.

She unlocked the door, pushed it open and he waited for her to enter. She turned to close the door on him.

He took a step inside to fulfill his promise to Darcie. "Could I get a glass of water before I head out?"

"Sure, of course." She stiffened, belying her generous words. "I should have thought to offer you one." She hung her coat on a hook and kicked off her shoes, visibly relaxing, and headed down a short hallway. She stopped to flick on a gas fireplace. "Have a seat, and I'll get your water."

He stepped into the room, the heat from the fire already warming the small area. The space had hardwood floors, white bead board and chunky moldings reminiscent of the period. The walls were beige, the furniture traditional with red accents. A tiny artificial tree with equally tiny sparkling white stars sat on a small table in the corner.

Perfection. Like from a magazine.

Not a place where people like Brady actually kicked back and lived. Watched a ballgame and got snack crumbs all over the floor. After seeing Morgan's designer clothing, he should have expected this. Just like Heather, his high school crush who had everything he didn't. Big house. Fancy car. Nice clothes. All of it contrasted with his double-wide trailer and hand-me-down or thrift store clothes. Back then, he'd been fool enough to think Heather actually liked him, but she'd shut him down faster than a bullet from his rifle. So would Morgan if he was crazy enough to follow this attraction.

Feeling like he could easily break the small sofa and chairs, he went to the window and stared onto the quiet street so in contrast with the shooting from earlier. His adrenaline had subsided and a headache was forming. He massaged his temples and tried to relax, but he felt jittery.

If Morgan's place wasn't so unbelievably clean, he'd pull out his knife and the small hunk of wood

that he always carried in his jacket pocket to whittle when he was left standing around.

A scream pierced the air. Shattering glass
followed.

The kitchen. Morgan.

Adrenaline rekindled in his veins. Hand on his
sidearm, he closed the distance to the kitchen in
a few strides. He stepped inside, his boots grinding over broken glass. Morgan stood by the sink,
physically unharmed, but her face was whiter than
the snow of a Minnesota blizzard from his childhood.

"Someone was here. He left—" Her words were
barely more than a whisper.

Brady turned off the running water and looked
around. He saw nothing odd other than the glass
she'd dropped on the floor. "Left what?"

"Those." She pointed at the countertop. "I didn't
leave them there."

Brady looked at the counter, then back at her
ashen face. His pulse kicked into high gear, and he
drew his weapon. It was a good thing he'd walked
Morgan home. A very good thing.

FOUR

Brady needed to check the other rooms for an intruder, but he also wanted to take a better look at the photograph lying under a long-stemmed red rose. He positioned his body so he could keep an eye on the door and still check out the picture.

The downright creepy photo was of an engagement announcement from the *Oregonian* newspaper. A man sat next to Morgan, but his body had been erased with a picture-editing program, leaving only a silhouette with the words Your One True Love superimposed on it. The caption below read, *You are mine. You will marry no one but me.*

"This looks like a real announcement that someone modified." He quickly checked her hand to see if he'd missed a big sparkling ring. Her finger was bare.

"It's from my engagement to Preston Hunter. I broke it off a few months ago. Apparently some sicko thinks it's funny." She stared at the counter.

"Not funny. Stalkerish."

A flash of horror widened her eyes. "You think I have a stalker?"

"That's what I aim to find out." He headed for the door.

"Wait," she called out, looking like she might be sick. "Where are you going?"

"I need to make sure no one else is in the apartment."

Grim realization dawned on her face. "You think whoever left this is still here."

"It's a good possibility. I didn't notice any signs of forced entry. Any chance this is a current boyfriend with a key who has a sick sense of humor and wanted to surprise you?" he asked, not liking the fact that she might be in a relationship.

"I don't have a boyfriend." She wrapped her arms around her slender waist.

"The message doesn't point to the former fiancé, but I have to ask. Is he mad that you ended things with him?"

She shook her head. "No."

"And no other boyfriends?" he asked again, to be sure.

"I haven't even dated since I broke off with Preston, and I haven't given anyone a key to my place except my parents."

So, stalker it is.

"Then stay put while I check it out. And don't move or you could cut your feet." Brady eyed her for a long moment to be sure she would follow his instructions.

"Be careful." She clutched her arms tighter and chewed her lip.

After the second shock of the night, he hated to leave her alone, but it would be foolish not to check for an intruder. A few strides across the hall and he was in a bedroom. The space was neat. Organized. The same colors as the family room. He checked the closet and under the bed, then made sure the windows were locked even though the apartment was on the fifth floor. He glanced into a small bathroom with a pedestal sink, claw-foot tub and subway tiles. Also empty.

He stepped to the front door and searched for any signs of forced entry. The wood was smooth and free from pry marks.

Odd. Very odd.

He dug out his phone, called Jake and relayed the incident so they could report it to the Portland Police Bureau. The FRS responded to emergencies across the entire city, but they didn't have jurisdiction to investigate crimes within city limits.

"I've got the detective's card from the shooting," Brady continued. "But I don't get the feeling that this is related to the train incident or another disgruntled plaintiff. Do you think I should call Rossi or should this be handled separately?"

Jake didn't answer right away. Brady knew he was thinking. Pondering. The usual Jake. He cleared his throat. "With no sign of forced entry, it seems more like you have a relationship gone bad. You really want to bother PPB this late at night with that?"

"Normally I'd agree with you, but Morgan says she doesn't have a boyfriend and hasn't dated in months. Plus, I'm getting a stalker vibe here."

A long hiss of air. "I'll have to call in favors to get a quick response so you'd better be right."

"Not sure I am, but then, her life could depend on us taking the right action here."

"You're right. Can't be too careful. I'll call the watch commander. Rossi is likely the detective on call and if he's finished at the scene, the commander will send him over. Otherwise you'll have to hang out there until someone else arrives."

Not a hardship, Brady thought and it surprised him. "I'm off tomorrow so I can stay as long as needed."

"I'll text you when I know something." Jake disconnected.

Brady kept his phone in hand so he wouldn't miss the text and returned to the kitchen. A hint of color had returned to Morgan's face, and she was talking on the phone to someone named Lacy. He suspected this was the woman who'd taken the train with Morgan. It sounded like they were good friends.

Not wanting to interrupt, he leaned against the counter and took the opportunity to study her while she was distracted. He couldn't put his finger on the word that best described her. Maybe *delicate*. Or *pampered*. Her features were fine, hence delicate, and her skin was creamy and flawless. Maybe from expensive beauty treatments. He could be wrong, of course, but he suspected she'd been pampered all her life.

His phone chimed, and he read a message from Darcie. You get Morgan home okay?

He didn't want to tell Darcie about this incident via text. He typed, In her apartment safe and sound.

He phone chimed another message and he switched to Jake's profile. Rossi on the way. ETA 5 minutes.

Perfect.

Morgan hung up, and glanced at him, seeming surprised to see him still standing there.

"Why don't we go into living room to talk about this?" He didn't give her a chance to respond but lifted her into his arms to carry her over the glass.

She pushed back and gaped at him. "What are you doing?"

"The glass. You'll cut your feet." As he continued walking, her scent wrapped around him. Soft, feminine. Fresh, like a spring breeze after the rain.

She scowled. "You could have gotten my shoes instead of taking over and manhandling me."

It was his turn to gape. "Manhandling? I'm simply helping you out."

The minute they hit the living room she squirmed out of his arms and planted her hands on her hips. "That kind of help I don't need." She stormed across the room, moving as far from him as possible.

He liked the fire in her eyes as she stared at him. Liked her animated expression. Liked that the vivid fear was gone from her face.

He glanced at his watch. Four minutes remaining until Rossi's arrival. If he continued to let his interest in her distract him, it'd be four very long minutes.

Distance and professionalism. That's what he needed.

He gestured at the sofa. "Let's sit down and talk about the rose and picture."

He expected an argument, but she perched on the edge of a red chair.

He took the far end of the sofa, feeling like a giant. He didn't know how to start this conversation other than bluntly stating his opinion. If she was lying, he'd soon know. "There was no sign of forced entry. Whoever left this surprise either had a key or is a master at picking locks."

"As I said, only my parents have a key." Her tone remained terse and irritated. "I suppose that means their live-in staff would have access, too, but I've had little to do with my family since I moved out of their guesthouse three months ago."

Live-in staff. Just as he'd suspected. Pampered.

He'd have to make sure Rossi knew about the staff. Maybe one of them had a thing for her or resented her. "Would you mind calling your parents to see if their keys are missing?"

"Mind?" Her eyes narrowed. "Honestly, yes. If my father hears about this, he'll drive over here and demand I move back home."

"At your age?"

She sighed, a long, drawn-out breath, her eyes lifting to the ceiling. "I think I could be headed for the retirement home, and as his only child, he'd still insist on taking care of me. By his definition, that means keeping me where he can see me."

"We need to know if they still have the keys or if they've been stolen and the intruder used them to gain access."

Her shoulders stiffened. "Then I'll have to call them, but only after I figure out what to say that doesn't bring Dad running over here."

"Okay, so give it some thought, but be sure you make that call tonight." Her response was a clipped nod so he moved on. "Is there a building superintendent or manager here, who might have a key?"

"Obviously the rental company would, but they're off-site."

"They could have had a break-in where keys were stolen, I suppose," Brady said, thinking aloud. "Though they'd likely inform you of such and replace your locks. Did you ever leave your keys unattended?"

"Unattended?" She chewed on her lip, something he was beginning to think was a habit. It was full and plump and far too distracting.

"You know," he rushed on, though no explanation was necessary. "You left the keys out where someone could get to them when you weren't watching."

She tapped her chin with a slender finger. "I suppose I've dropped the ring on my desk at work. Who doesn't do that? But I'm sure no one took them long enough to get a duplicate made."

He wished. "Unfortunately, keys can now be duplicated by sending a digital picture to an online locksmith."

"You're kidding, right? They just have to take a picture?" Fear widened her eyes. She seemed even more vulnerable, tempting him to cross the room to take her hand.

He planted himself more firmly on the sofa instead. "I'm afraid it's true. That's why I need you to think of any place you could've set the keys down long enough for someone to snap a picture."

She tapped her chin again, her fingernail painted a light pink and perfectly manicured. "Work, like I said. And the gym."

"You leave your keys unattended at the gym?"

"Not really. Just set them on the bench in the locker room as I dress. Or on the counter when signing in and out, but from what you say that's long enough." She stared at him. "I've left them out at church, too, though I doubt anyone there would do this."

"You never know."

She arched a perfectly plucked brow. "I doubt it."

Fine, she didn't believe him. Most people wouldn't, but he saw people at their worst and knew what they were capable of. He also suspected the ex-fiancé had been alone with her keys at some point, but the message didn't lead Brady to believe this Preston guy had left the note.

"So how do we find out who might have a key?" she asked.

We? There's no we *here.* "I've arranged for Rossi to come over. He'll be here any minute to take your statement and go from there."

"What?" She laughed. "Aren't you a police officer? Can't you handle this—wait." She covered her mouth for a moment, then circled her arms around her waist. "You think this is related to Craig. That it's not over."

He held up his hands. "Slow down. I'm not saying that at all. It's just a jurisdictional matter. I'm County and you live in Portland's city limits. It's the Portland Police Bureau's responsibility to investigate this incident."

"Oh," she said, sounding disappointed. "Does that mean you'll be leaving?"

"I'll wait for Rossi and make sure you're in good hands before I leave."

As if on cue, the doorbell rang. Morgan startled.

"Relax. I'm sure it's Rossi."

She started to rise.

"I'll let him in." Brady shot to his feet before she could get up. "Do you have a photocopier?"

"On my printer, why?"

"You should make a copy of the threats you received. Then you can give the file to Rossi so he can get started on it ASAP."

"Oh, right, okay."

Brady headed for the door. She'd have plenty of time to make the copies as he intended to have a conversation with Rossi before the other man entered the apartment. It would be better if this conversation happened without Morgan, because Brady suspected without evidence of an intrusion, Rossi would think Morgan was lying about not having any relationships gone bad. And if Rossi thought the items were from a disgruntled ex-boyfriend, he wouldn't take this threat seriously, leaving her in potential danger. Relationships gone bad made people say stupid things—sometimes even do stupid things like leaving a rose and note for the former girlfriend—but it was less common for actual physical harm to occur.

Brady grabbed the doorknob. An image of a man turning the same knob flashed into his brain. A sick man, focused on Morgan. Doing everything necessary to gain her affection. Stalking. Hunting when she was alone. Unprotected.

What if Rossi blew her off like Brady suspected? Left her to fend for herself?

Brady couldn't let that happen. Wouldn't let that happen despite his desire to put distance between them. This was no longer about a promise to Darcie to see Morgan home. About guilt for hesitating to pull the trigger. This was about a woman's life. Plain and simple.

If he couldn't convince Rossi to help Morgan, he'd have no choice. He'd force down these feelings that kept surfacing around her and step in. She could count on him to be by her side and keep her safe.

Waiting for Brady to return with the detective, Morgan shoved her phone into her pocket and sent the threat letters feeding into the printer. She'd called her mother and learned that the keys were right where her father had left them. She'd also managed to raise her mother's suspicions, but Morgan had avoided telling her the truth. If her dad had answered, it might have been a different story.

Morgan listened to the hum of the copier and looked around the room she'd so carefully decorated. The space was neutral on purpose. No photos. No mementos from time spent with her family, which would only remind her of their disagreement about where she should live.

She'd planned this place as a sanctuary. A symbol of her new independence. Now each shadowed corner held fear. Her space had been violated. Along with it, so had she. Again. For the second time tonight.

Stress weighed heavily on her and nausea formed in the pit of her stomach. Stress. When she'd worked on the lawsuit, the stress had left her with daily nausea. So many people had depended on her back then. Her father. Preston. The mill workers who would lose their jobs if she lost the case. Despite feeling sick, she'd dug deep for the strength she needed to go on. She did her duty, then broke free of her father's desire to keep her employed at the mill. She'd formed her own life, and her stomach had settled down. Even when her father basically disowned her.

She'd just started to enjoy life and now this? It was almost too much to bear.

"Why, God?" she whispered. *Isn't my father disowning me enough? Do You have to take my new start in life, too? My peace?*

Okay, fine, she got that God didn't actually take her peace. She let the fear take over and steal it. But after her night, how could she not?

She heard a noise in the bedroom and jumped. She knew it was the old building groaning with age as it often did, but still, the room suddenly seemed oppressive without Brady. She didn't want to admit to needing anyone. Would never admit it aloud, but his presence had kept the panic at bay.

Despite what common sense told her, she hurried to the front door and slipped into her shoes before jerking it open. Brady stood, his feet planted wide, his shoulders back like a tower of strength. She was reluctant to lean on him, but she needed him to get through this.

Tonight only, she told herself as joined the men. *Tonight only*.

"Ms. Thorsby." Rossi stepped forward and ran a wide thumb over the doorjamb.

"Please call me Morgan."

He gave a clipped nod. "As Owens said, there's no sign of forced entry." Instead of looking at Brady, he eyed Morgan, his eyebrow raised, as if she'd done something wrong. She didn't like his attitude, but didn't know what to say so she said nothing.

"Show me the rose and picture," he said, his voice almost accusatory.

He seemed to be blaming her for this. Or was he mad at having to stay out all night? Regardless, she wouldn't let the surly bear of a guy intimidate her. She'd state her case and keep to the point so she didn't waste his time.

"Follow me." She led the way to the kitchen. Rossi stomped behind her and Brady's lighter footsteps sounded farther behind. She dreaded entering the kitchen with slivers of glass so representative of the shards of unease she felt, but she had to be strong.

She stepped in, picking her way through the glass, and turned to face Rossi, who stared at the rose and picture. Brady moved to the far side of the room and rested against the counter. She couldn't get a read on his mood, but then he'd be going home in a little bit, so it didn't much matter.

She focused on Rossi. "I've already told Deputy Owens that I don't have a boyfriend and haven't dated in the last few months."

"This picture looks like a real announcement," he said.

She stifled a sigh at having to tell her story again and quickly brought Rossi up to speed.

"Other than property management, my parents are the only people with a key," she added. "I just talked to my mother. She confirmed the keys are in my dad's desk drawer right where they keep them. They obviously wouldn't do this, so this person got into my apartment another way."

Rossi looked her straight in the eyes. "Are you suggesting a secret admirer, then?"

"It's the only explanation. Unless of course, a plaintiff from the trial is trying a different way to scare me."

"Doesn't feel like that to me," Brady spoke for the first time.

"I'd have to agree. More like a jilted lover or a

boyfriend wannabe." Rossi frowned. "Still, I can't fully rule out a connection to the lawsuit. Shaw's behind bars, but until now we had no reason to check his whereabouts before the shooting. I'll investigate, and once you provide the other threats you've received, I'll review them to see if there's a connection."

"I made copies so you can take them with you."

Rossi gestured at the floor. "The glass?"

"I dropped it when I saw the picture."

Rossi pulled out a small notepad and pen. "Tell me more about this engagement. You said the guy's name is Preston Hunter, right?"

She nodded, and he jotted it down.

"I honestly don't think he did this," she continued. "He's moved on and is already engaged." *Plus he's a white rose kind of person*, she thought but didn't add.

"You'd be surprised what guys might do," Rossi said. "I've seen it all. Tell me more about Preston."

Rossi was barking up the wrong tree, but she'd answer his questions so they could get to how he was going to find this stalker. "He comes from a well-respected family. They own Orion Transport. Our family businesses work hand in hand so we go way back. In fact, I've known him since we were children. It was natural for us to start dating and get engaged."

"Why'd you break up?" Brady asked, surprising her for a moment. She hadn't realized that he was still standing there.

"We weren't compatible." She crossed her arms and hoped he'd leave it at that.

"How so?" His gaze remained fixed on her, direct and searching.

So much for hoping he'd let it go. "I'm more laid-back. He's controlling." The desire to explain her actions had her opening her mouth to continue, but then she clamped it closed. Neither Brady nor Rossi had a reason to know about Preston's incessant need to plan her life and activities.

Both Rossi and Brady's eyebrows rose.

"No, wait," she said. "If you're thinking there's something sinister there, you're wasting your time. I still see Preston on occasion when I visit my parents, and we are completely cordial. And, like I said, he has a new fiancée. Someone far more suited to him than I was."

"And her name is?"

"Natasha something. Sorry, I don't remember her last name."

Rossi scribbled something in his notepad then shifted on his feet. "And you really haven't dated anyone else since then?"

"No."

Rossi tapped his pen against the paper. "No one. Not a single guy. Really?"

"Really." She tightened her arms and tried to hold on to her temper.

"You're an attractive woman, Morgan, so that's hard to believe." Rossi turned to Brady. "Isn't that hard to believe, Owens?"

"Yes," Brady said, his gaze fixed on her. "But then, I've seen how strong willed she is and if she set her mind against dating, I suspect she would succeed."

Searching for a response, she looked at Brady. "You don't have a ring on your finger. How many women have you dated in the last few months?"

"Darcie fixed me up a couple of times. I tried to get out of them, but she's kind of pushy." He frowned. "If not for her, I wouldn't have gone on a date, either."

Morgan switched her focus to Rossi. "Brady's single and attractive. Does it surprise you that he hasn't been dating?"

"Don't know about how attractive he is," he scowled. "But we're not talking about Owens, here. He isn't claiming someone left a surprise in his apartment."

"Claiming?" The word shot out, ending Morgan's plan to keep to the point. "You don't believe me, do you? You think I staged this for some reason."

"Honestly?" Rossi arched a brow as the charged air hung between them. "Your story rings false. I'm more inclined to believe you had a fight with a boyfriend, and now you want him to get in trouble so you call us with a bogus story."

She planted her hands on her hips. "I did no such thing, and I certainly hope you're planning to investigate my complaint."

"Frankly," he said flipping his notebook closed, "I'm not. There's no proof of a break-in and our resources are stretched thin already…"

"Hold up," Brady stepped in. "You can at least canvass the neighbors and dust for prints. Maybe talk to the management company."

Rossi scowled at Brady, but Morgan smiled her thanks at him.

"That I can do, but you should know, every minute I spend on this takes time away from looking into the other threats that have been made against you."

"That's obviously a priority," Brady said.

Rossi held up a hand. "Don't worry. I understand and I'll do my part. Just know that I have a lot on my plate right now. So I'll grab my fingerprint kit and get started." He stepped out of the kitchen.

Morgan sighed out her frustration. She caught sight of the rose again. Red and threatening against the white countertop. Like blood. Vivid and terrifying. A sharp jolt of fear stabbed through her. She looked at Brady, found his focus fixed on her.

"Are you going to leave now?" Her voice caught as she asked.

"I'll stay until Rossi finishes up," he replied.

"Thank you," she whispered in relief.

She hated that she sounded weak. Hated *feeling* weak, but she hated the thought of being alone even more. For the first time since she'd moved into her apartment, she wondered why she'd ever been so desperate to be alone.

FIVE

Morgan slung the straps for her briefcase and gym bag over her shoulders and stepped to the door. Fear that had plagued her all night made her hesitate and her hand lingered on the knob. "You're being ridiculous. No one's waiting to hurt you."

She pulled her shoulders back and stepped outside. Wind howled down the tree-lined street, but the sun shone bright and the snow was melting. She huddled into her coat and carefully made her way down the slippery sidewalk. A nutty scent drifted up from the coffee shop on the lower level of her building. Her salary left little money to spend on coffee, and she rarely did, but after her lack of sleep and the unusually cold morning she couldn't resist the aroma.

She took the steps down to the shop and ordered a large mocha with whipped cream. She'd have to work harder tonight at the gym to burn off the extra calories, but after her day yesterday she deserved a treat.

The barista was efficient and Morgan was soon pressing the remote for her car. She checked for oncoming cars on the busy street as she sipped her coffee, the chocolaty goodness sliding down her throat and leaving a warm trail. Traffic cleared for a moment and she quickly opened the door before another car could charge past and sideswipe her door. Her gaze landed on the driver's seat. She jumped back in horror. The coffee cup dropped from her hand, exploding on the pavement, darkening the brilliant white snow and splashing up her leg. She yelped at the pain but even that couldn't take her eyes from the seat.

Two long-stemmed red roses crossed like an X lay on the seat, an envelope beneath them. She was curious about what the envelope contained, but the roses captured her thoughts. Maybe the X meant something, maybe not. Didn't matter. What mattered was that someone broke into her car without damaging it. No broken windows. No jimmied lock. The roses were fresh, as if they'd just come from a garden or a cooler, not been exposed to freezing temperatures for hours. They'd been left recently, which meant her stalker had to be close.

She fired a look down the street, searching for anyone watching her. Two people headed for their cars. No one looked at her. At least, no one standing out in the open.

Could her stalker be hiding in the bushes across the street—behind trees down the road—while she stood out here? Vulnerable. Her life in danger.

A car horn sounded behind her, and she spun around, clutching her briefcase like a shield. A man sat behind the wheel of his car. His gaze frustrated, he made shooing gestures with his hands.

Feeling as if she was coming out of a fog, she looked around. She'd backed into traffic, but she didn't care. Could she ask this man for his help? Ask to sit with him while she called 911? Could she even trust this man? Was he the stalker?

You're still vulnerable. Move, now. Go. Quickly.

She slammed her car door and ran for her apartment building. She frantically slid her fingers along the ring to locate the right key for the main entrance. Her hand trembled. The key refused to fit the lock. A noise from behind startled her. The keys flew from her hand as she shot a look over her shoulder. Spotted a woman walking her fluffy white dog down the street.

Not a threat, but one still existed. She had to get inside. She scrambled to find the right key. Got it into the lock and twisted.

Now what? The thought came unbidden. *With the rose and photo left on the counter, you're no safer inside.*

You're not safe anywhere.

* * *

Brady's phone rang, dragging him out of a deep sleep. He groaned and glanced at the clock. Better be important for someone to get him out of bed at 6:00 a.m. when he'd stayed with Rossi until two o'clock. Fat lot of good it did them. They'd lifted a few fingerprints but located no other leads.

He grabbed his phone and when he saw the caller ID, he was instantly alert.

"Morgan," he answered. "Is something wrong?"

"Roses," she whispered. "Two of them. In my car with an envelope."

A vision of her standing near her vehicle, a dangerous stalker nearby, had Brady lurching to his feet and grabbing a pair of jeans. "Where are you?"

"In the coffee shop of my building. I thought staying in a public place would be the most secure location right now so I hurried down here."

"Stay there. I'm on my way."

"Thank you, Brady." He heard the relief in her voice, and he hated to admit it, but he liked that she'd called him to come to her rescue.

He pulled on a T-shirt and quickly brushed his teeth, then grabbing his jacket on the way out, he made a mad dash down the stairs to his ancient pickup truck. One set of footprints led across the asphalt to Jake's car.

"Brady?" he called out.

"It's Morgan. More roses," he explained and

jumped into his truck. He used the wipers to clear the snowy windshield and coaxed the ancient truck to start in the unusual cold. On the road, Brady called Rossi who was even grumpier than last night, but he agreed to meet Brady at Morgan's car.

Rush hour had begun, but with the snow, most people would stay home until later, allowing Brady to pull up to the coffee shop in less than ten minutes. He grabbed latex gloves from his console and headed over to talk to Morgan, searching the area for potential threats on the way.

He didn't like what he saw. Plenty of places for a stalker to hide on the street and watch Morgan's movements. No way would he bring her out into the open like this. He'd insist Morgan remain in the shop while he checked her car.

She met him at the door. Dressed in another suit that appeared tailor-made, this one blue, she looked professional, but it was the fear darkening her eyes that struck him hard.

"Thank you for coming," she said, sounding like he'd arrived at a social event instead of another invasion into her life.

Part of Brady was impressed that she could control her emotions, the other part was mad that she was hiding her real feelings. Still, her body language told the story. Arms clutched around her waist. Leaning forward as if she might drop any minute. Her face pale. Her hands trembling.

"Tell me exactly what you found," he said, making sure he sounded comforting and reassuring.

She flicked a gaze outside then quickly back at him, the fear stronger now. "I stopped for coffee, then unlocked my car with the remote. When I opened the door, I found two roses lying in an X pattern and sitting on top of a white linen envelope."

Likely another picture. "This X pattern mean anything to you?"

She shook her head.

"And the envelope?"

"I didn't open it. I was too afraid." She was shaking, and looked like she'd melt to the floor.

He took her elbow and moved her to a chair. She looked up at him, seeming small and defenseless.

He wanted to rail at the injustice heaped on her head, but he held it together by shoving his hands into his pockets. "Did you notice anything else?

She stared off into the distance. "The windows weren't broken or the doors jimmied. I guess he could have used one of those bar things I see on TV shows, but since my key is on the same ring as my apartment key, he likely made a copy of that one, too." She paused and chewed on her lip for a moment.

"Anyone else have your car key? Do you keep a spare set hidden somewhere?"

"Just at my parents. No other spare set."

"Have you checked with them to see if anyone stole the keys overnight?"

"I called my mom right after you. They're still in the drawer." She looked like she wanted to add something but stared over his shoulder instead.

He followed her gaze through the street level window. "Which vehicle is yours?"

"I'll show you." She started to rise.

"No." He stopped her with a gentle hand on her shoulder. "You stay here. It's safer."

She jerked free and cast him a defiant look. She was suddenly all fire and passion, much like last night. He watched, enjoying the metamorphosis from timid victim to fierce warrior and waited for her to refuse his directive. He didn't like the thought of her rushing out onto the street, but he respected her determination in the face of danger.

She kept eye contact with him for a long while until she finally sighed, her agitation disappearing with it. She dug her keys from a leather briefcase, then handed them to him. "It's the blue BMW. Three cars behind your truck." Panic returned to her eyes.

So she'd let her fear take over enough that she'd been watching for his arrival. A protective feeling surged to the surface and the urge to touch her was strong. She needed reassurance. Needed to know that he'd be there for her. Any hour of the day. The minute she called.

Not a good idea. She should call Rossi instead.

Brady shoved his hands into his pockets and smiled to ease her fear. "You hang tight. I'll be right back."

Outside, he fought through the biting wind as he passed his truck to get to the sleek BMW. Talk about contrasts. Battered and rusty from Minnesota winters, his pickup was on its last legs. Her Beemer, a metallic blue coupe that Brady recognized as the top-of-the-line, was polished and shiny. *Of course.* He should have known by now that she'd have nothing less than the best.

Snapping on gloves, he clicked the lock. He noted a paper cup lying by the front wheel, the snow tinted with chocolaty coffee. He suspected Morgan had dropped it as she'd dropped the glass last night. Another shock to her system.

He leaned inside the spotlessly clean vehicle. Perfect, like her apartment. Just as she'd said, two red roses lay on the leather seat and were positioned in an X shape, which was unusual, but what really drew his attention was the freshness of the flowers. The temperature had dropped well below freezing last night, and if the roses had been inside long they'd be damaged.

He lifted the envelope and dread filled his gut even before he opened it. He pulled out an official-looking invitation printed on quality paper. It wasn't engraved, but printed on a laser printer.

He read the front page, inviting the recipient to a wedding celebration. Inside, the details claimed Morgan Thorsby would marry Her One True Love. Grimacing, Brady scanned down the page to the date.

Saturday. Only five days away.

Could this creep be planning to abduct her on that date to force her to marry him?

Crazy. Totally crazy. And dangerous.

Brady's stomach churned. He had less than five days to find the stalker before this jerk harmed Morgan. Hopefully the car contained a lead. He took his time, looking through the front, in the glove box, under the seats, in the back, the trunk. Came up empty.

He was starting for the coffee shop when Rossi pulled up. He double-parked, proving he wasn't intending to stay long.

"Owens," he said and stepped to the driver's door where he made a cursory inspection of the vehicle. "No forced entry again."

"No," Brady said. "And I searched the entire vehicle. Nothing."

"At least we know where Shaw is and he couldn't have planted the roses." Rossi stood staring at the car. "You getting the same vibe about this as I am?"

"Depends on what vibe you're getting."

Rossi looked at Brady. "Bored little rich girl. Decides to invent a stalker to get back at an ex who jilted her."

Brady stepped back. He'd been thinking of

Morgan as a little rich girl, too, but his anger rose at Rossi's tone. Why, he didn't know. The guy was right. She was rich, maybe pampered. Maybe spoiled.

Brady was trained to read people. He did it all day long on the job. Read them, predicted what they might do, then acted accordingly. Morgan was many things, things he didn't want to dwell on now, but he'd spent enough time with her to see she wasn't an attention seeker and he trusted his gut instinct.

"I'm more inclined to believe her," he said making sure his tone carried his conviction.

Rossi arched his brow. "She tell you something I'm not getting from the scene?"

"No. Her story was simple. She opened the car door. The roses and invitation were here."

"Odd that they're so fresh. Not wilted from the cold, right? Seems unlikely that the stalker put them here in broad daylight. Means she could've left them."

No. The word shot into Brady's brain but he held back from saying it. If he was going to get Rossi fully on board, he'd needed proof of Morgan's actions this morning. Maybe a video. Brady searched for surveillance cameras on the nearby buildings. Found none. So what else could prove her innocence? A money trail.

"You could pull Morgan's financials to see if she's bought any flowers lately," Brady offered.

Rossi rolled his eyes. "Credit card receipts for three roses? Nah. She could've paid cash."

He was right and Brady was grasping at straws here, but he wouldn't give up easily. "What about showing her picture at local flower shops? See if anyone recognizes her or they have invoices for a purchase?"

"Same thing. Flowers can be bought just about everywhere these days. And if she was trying to hide the purchase, she'd make sure she got them from an untraceable source, like a street vendor."

"Your points are all valid, but you can't just ignore the fact that she might have a stalker."

"I'm not ignoring it. If I was, I would've gotten a whole lot more sleep last night, but after you took off, I brought the fingerprints to our tech, and I also confirmed the ex-fiancé is in Florida."

"You're sure he's out of town?"

"Positive." Rossi frowned. "I'd honestly hoped the guy was behind this so I could close the case and move on. Being the jilted boyfriend and all, I thought it was likely, but I was wrong." He blew out a long breath and stared at the car. "I'll dust for prints again. We can compare any we find to last night's prints and search AFIS for a match. I'll do a canvass again and review the threat file she gave me, but after that I'm done unless something else turns up."

Brady wanted him to do more than search the Automated Fingerprint Identification System—a national fingerprint and criminal history system managed by the FBI—but had to agree that there was nothing more to do. "I appreciate you taking this seriously."

Rossi nodded gravely. "I suggest Morgan gets her locks changed."

Brady agreed. "She's in the coffee shop. I'll arrange that with her while you check for prints."

Wearily, Rossi ran his hand down his face. "I'll be in to take her statement in a minute."

Brady turned on his heel and jogged down the steps to the shop. Morgan met him at the door again, her expression hopeful.

"Rossi's dusting for prints." Brady gestured at a table. "We should sit. It'll take some time."

She looked at her watch and shook her head. "I have an important presentation this morning and can't be late. With my car out of commission I'll have to take MAX so I should get going."

"If we want Rossi to continue to take this seriously, you need to stay to give him your statement."

"I want to stay." She glanced outside then back at Brady. "But my clients are counting on me to obtain the support of a local employer today, which could mean more jobs." She tapped the screen on her phone and Brady saw the MAX timetable appear. "I have to leave right now to catch MAX. I'm sorry if I brought you out here for nothing, but my clients come first."

"You can take my truck if you like." What was he thinking offering his rusty old pickup? Not that he expected Ms. Uptown Girl to even consider it.

"I couldn't put you out," she replied, but he could see she was thinking about his offer. Interesting to say the least.

He should let it drop, but now he wanted to see how she would react once she got a closer look at the truck. "I'm off today so I can wait around while Rossi finishes the canvass. Then I'll stop by your office to give you an update and deliver your keys." *Make sure you're all right in case you need me again.*

"On your day off? I already got you up at the crack of dawn. I couldn't ask you to do more."

"No biggie."

"You're sure you don't mind?"

He gestured at the counter. "I've got coffee, muffins and free Wi-Fi. What's to mind?"

"Then, yes," she said with a smile that lightened her face and gave her a carefree look.

He felt a goofy grin take over his mouth. He could stand just like this for hours. Watching her. Enjoying her smile. Exactly the kind of thing he needed to be alert for if he spent any time with her. "I'll just grab that coffee. Can I get you anything?"

She shook her head.

He gestured at a table. "Then have a seat, and we can talk about this until you have to leave."

While she perched on the edge of a chair like a bird ready to take flight, he quickly ordered black coffee and two huge banana nut muffins from the perky barista. At the table, he moved a chair so he could see the door.

He concentrated on peeling the paper from his muffin, thinking his questions might be easier for her to answer without him staring at her the way he'd been doing. With a stalker after her, she probably felt like she had too many eyes on her already. "I think it's time to ask who besides your parents might have access to the drawer with your keys."

"The staff, of course. And Dad takes meetings in his home office sometimes, but I don't know who he's met with in the last few months."

"Can we find out?"

"Maybe my mom will tell me, but my dad's pretty tight-lipped about his business dealings."

"Check with your mom and let me know what you learn." He moved on. "I suggest you change the locks for your apartment and car. I can arrange it for you while you're at work, if you want."

She narrowed her eyes and studied him. "Why would you do that for me?"

"You need help." He bit into his muffin.

"Nothing else?" She held his gaze for a long moment, distrust rampant in her expression. "No hidden agenda?"

Suspicious little thing. "No agenda other than

to help you." He smiled to reassure her. "I'm trying to do the whole knight-in-shining-armor thing. Maybe not real well, though, as you seem awfully suspicious of me."

She let out a breath, her defensive posture relaxing. "I'm sorry. It's not you. In the world I come from, people rarely do things for others without an ulterior motive."

He'd always thought the rich and famous had it so easy, but maybe that lifestyle wasn't everything it was cracked up to be. She'd left it behind, after all. At least, that's what she'd been saying, but the expensive car, swank apartment and fine clothes said differently.

The door opened. A cold draft swept over them as Rossi stepped inside.

"Ms. Thorsby," he said in greeting. He took a chair, turned it around and straddled it, then dug out his notebook and pen. "Tell me what happened this morning."

Brady sat back to finish his muffin and sip the dark-roasted coffee as Morgan told her story. She'd erected a wall of confidence for Rossi, and her emotions seemed firmly under control again. Maybe she'd gotten over her fear, or maybe she felt more comfortable around Brady and wasn't afraid to let him see her distress. He hoped that was true. It would make him feel better about the way she'd managed to get past the defenses he'd put up. To make him interested in her when she was the last woman on Earth that he should be having such thoughts about.

Rossi snapped his notebook closed. "I've lifted a few prints from the car and should have time to run them later today. Where can I reach you if I need you?"

She dug a business card from her bulging leather briefcase and wrote a phone number on the back. "My cell." She slid it across the table then passed another card to Brady. "You'll need this for my work address." She stood. "Thank you for your help, Detective. Now I really need to get to work."

Brady got up, too. "I'll walk you out."

Rossi nodded at the barista. "I might as well grab a cup of coffee while I'm here. With the snow, it'll be a crazy day at the precinct."

Morgan picked up her gym bag and briefcase. Brady reached out to carry them for her, but she held fast and headed for the door. As fragile as she seemed at times, she was tough to the core. He appreciated her strength, but honestly, it was starting to irritate him, too. She needed help right now, his help, and he wished she'd just accept it without questioning his motives.

He stopped in front of her. "Let me make a quick sweep before you go outside." He expected an argument but got a clipped nod instead. *Good.* At least she wasn't too stubborn to listen to common sense.

On the street, he ran his gaze up and down, checking trees, shrubbery and between cars. Rossi had pulled his car out of traffic, but other than that, nothing had changed. He gestured for Morgan to join him. They started down the sidewalk, and he rested his hand on his sidearm just in case he'd missed something in his search. At his truck, he unlocked the door and stepped back.

Morgan set her bags on the cracked vinyl seat, then gracefully settled behind the wheel, looking as uncomfortable as a regal princess at a thrift shop. He was suddenly very aware of how completely run-down his truck was. He kept it clean. No trash or fast food wrappers like a lot of guys, but it had seen better days. Honestly, it was about ready for the scrap metal yard. He risked a glance at her face, expecting disgust. Instead, he found that iron mask she was able to call up at a moment's notice.

He gave her the keys and rested an arm on the door. "She likes to stall sometimes, but she always starts back up."

Morgan raised an eyebrow. "She?"

"Aw, come on, don't tell me people in your life never gave their vehicles a name."

"Never. At least, not that I know of."

"Sounds like you've been hanging around the wrong kind of people," he said, though actually he was kind of embarrassed.

A tight smile broke the tense lines on her face.

"Thank you again for the loan of your truck. My presentation should be finished by noon. We can meet then."

She put the key in the ignition before looking back at him. "Her name. You didn't say."

"Bessie."

"Bessie?"

He should never have brought it up. Now he'd have to explain. "When I was in middle school I hung out at a friend's farm. Travis and I raised a calf for exhibit at the state fair. We named her Bessie after a cow we saw in TV commercials for a local milk company."

Memories of one of the best times of his life came rushing back and he allowed his thoughts to remain on caring for the animal. Bessie listened to all of his struggles and never judged. Plus, caring for her gave him hours and hours out in the fresh air. An escape from the tin can of a trailer they lived in. And then there was the unending food supplied by Travis's family. Until… The memories evaporated like a popped balloon. "After it was over, they sold her."

Morgan slid the seat forward. "So you named your truck in honor of the cow."

"Yeah." He felt his face flush in embarrassment at the silly sentiment.

"Don't be embarrassed. I think it's a very sweet thing to do." She gave his hand a quick squeeze.

Uncomfortable at letting her into a part of his life he'd never shared with others, he pulled back.

"Don't worry, I get it." A sweet smile softened her face as she adjusted the mirrors. "You have to be the big, tough deputy and can't let anyone see your true feelings." She winked at him. "Your secret is safe with me."

That wasn't the whole reason for his discomfort, but he didn't dispute her assumption and stood back while she fired up the engine. It coughed a few times, then caught and roared to life. The engine idled high, and Morgan's body vibrated on the seat until she put the shift into Drive and took off.

He continued to stand there, his gaze following the truck down the road, his mind on the fancy lady and his run-down truck. She claimed she'd left her other life behind and maybe she had. But he doubted driving a rusted bucket of bolts was what she meant, and he doubted she could ever get used to a life that included a heap of a truck. Translated, she could never get used to a guy like him.

SIX

Brady approached the PEA office. A storefront at the end of an older strip mall, the place was unassuming and slightly tattered. Not even the melting blanket of snow made it look more appealing.

He stepped inside and scanned the large front room. Computers lined one wall, photocopiers and printers another. Two men and a woman sat at one of three round tables, flipping through binders. Bulletin boards with motivational posters lined the back wall with a large desk sitting below.

Spotting him, a young woman with a cautious expression came around the desk. Where Morgan was fragile and delicate, this woman was sturdy and muscular. Her nametag read Lacy Sutton, likely the friend on the train with Morgan last night.

She forced a smile. "Can I help you?"

"I'm Brady Owens. I'm looking for Morgan."

She appraised him. "I was expecting you. Morgan's told me all about you."

He could only imagine what she might have said.

"I hope some of it was good," he joked.

"All of it." She smiled in earnest this time.

Brady relaxed. "Is the presentation over?"

"The meeting just broke up, and she's saying goodbye to our guests." Lacy nodded at the tables. "If you want to have a seat, I'll go tell Morgan you're here."

Brady took a chair at an empty table, and Lacy disappeared through a doorway in the back. As soon as she was gone, the job seekers started chatting about Morgan and the jobs program. Wondering if one of her clients might be her stalker, he listened in. With her good looks, it would be easy for a client to fall for her, and a client wouldn't likely come right out and admit his feelings. Especially if he was unemployed. He was more likely to take the secret admirer approach. Brady made a mental note to ask Morgan about her clients.

She soon entered the room and escorted four men in business suits to the front door. After shaking hands with them, she nodded a quick greeting for Brady and went straight to the job seekers.

She smiled and bent over the table. "How's it going today? Any new leads?"

The seekers looked at her with respect and each of them shared about the progress in their job search. As she interacted with the trio, her face glowed and her whole being came alive. He could see she truly cared about them and that they were genuinely thankful for her assistance. When she turned to Brady, the same smile lit her face, and he felt time stop for a moment. As much as he simply wanted to sit there and bask in her radiating warmth, he needed to get moving on finding her stalker. But he could ease into the topic and not totally annihilate her good mood.

"Does the smile mean your presentation went well, or you're happy to see me?"

"Both, actually," she said, then looked down.

Wow. He didn't expect her to admit she was glad to see him. "Can we go somewhere private to talk about this morning's event?"

Her smile vanished.

Nice one. Way to sugarcoat that and ease into the topic of the stalker.

"My cubicle is right this way." Her shoulders back, she led him through the back door. She stopped to pick up her briefcase and tote bag sitting just inside the door. "Thanks again for loaning me your truck. I got here just in time to drop my bags on the floor and run into the presentation."

"You're welcome," he said, but didn't attempt to take her bags this time.

They moved down a hallway to an area filled with cubicles and the chatter of busy workers. She entered a messy break room where she grabbed a bottle of thick liquid from the refrigerator. He assumed she planned to drink the orange gunk, but the color turned his stomach.

"I usually have one of these for energy in the morning, but with my meeting I didn't get a chance." She held it up. "It's a veggie/berry drink that I make. Would you like one?"

He mocked a shudder.

"Ah, not into healthy eating, huh?" She shook the bottle.

"Give me a big cheeseburger, a plate of fries, maybe some onion rings and an ice-cold root beer, and I'm set. Well, maybe add some deep-fried cheese curds into the mix, too."

She looked up laughing. "Are you serious about the curds?

"A Midwest thing. Born and raised in Minnesota."

She poured the drink into a glass and the liquid reminded him of sewage sludge. "I thought I heard that accent in your voice."

"Oh, ya, sure and you betcha." He mocked his Norwegian ancestry.

She grinned as she held up the glass. "You sure you don't want one?"

"I'll pass."

"You don't know what you're missing. It's a blend of tomato, broccoli, apple and carrots. A perfect energy drink."

He tried not to grimace but didn't manage it. "I'll take your word for it."

"Coward." She laughed. "There's a water cooler in the corner if you'd like some water."

"I'm good," he said.

She shifted the straps for her bags on her shoulder, headed for the door and started chugging the drink the way a person stranded in a desert might gulp down water. This behavior seemed so out of character for her usual genteel manners.

She'd finished the entire drink by the time they reached her cubicle. She came to a sudden stop. Brady couldn't react fast enough to keep from bumping into her. He shot an arm around her waist to stop her from taking a nosedive. He expected her to push free, but she clamped a hand over her mouth and pointed at the desk.

Brady followed the direction of her finger and found three red roses and another picture lying on her pristine desk.

"Not again." Brady's arm instinctively tightened around her.

She tried to swivel free but he was holding her too tightly. He relaxed his grip just enough to allow her turn, but he couldn't make himself release her.

"Who could be doing this?" She lifted her stricken gaze to his.

"Don't worry. We'll find out," he said, but he had no reason at this point to believe they would.

"I'm so thankful for your help." A tremulous smile found her lips.

Hoping to put her at ease, he smiled back at her.

She suddenly seemed to notice he was holding her, and she pushed against his chest to free herself. The warmth of her touch sent his senses firing and his pulse racing. He didn't want to let go, but short of making a fool of himself, he had no other choice but to release her.

After dropping her bags on the desk, she reached for the picture.

"Don't touch it," he warned.

She snapped her hand back and bent closer to look. She suddenly gasped and lurched back. "He was in my bedroom. Oh, no. No, no, no."

Knowing he wasn't going to like what he saw, Brady moved closer to get a better look at a picture of Morgan taken from above. A shadow of the man who took the photo fell over her as she peacefully slept in her bed. Superimposed in bright red letters on the bottom of the picture was the sentence, *We'll soon be together forever, my love.*

Rage roared up and threatened to choke Brady. He raised his fist, ready to slam it into the desk, but it would increase Morgan's fear. He tightened his fingers and faced her.

She bent forward, clutching her stomach. Her face was ashen, her lips pinched and glassy-eyed shock consumed her eyes.

He quickly blocked her view of the picture and

roses. "I take it since you went straight to the conference room that you're discovering this picture for the first time."

"I hadn't...I...I—" She dropped into her chair.

"So it could have been left last night or put here after you arrived today."

Her gaze bounced around the area as if she was trying to focus. "I guess so. Does this mean it's someone I work with?"

"Could be, but if the lock was picked at your apartment, your stalker could have gotten in here the same way. Is there a security system for the building?"

"No."

He stepped outside her cubicle and searched the large room. "No security cameras?"

"Not that I know of." Her focus was locked on the picture again.

He used the hem of his shirt to flip it over. "Tell me your exact steps when you arrived today."

She looked a bit green around the gills and swallowed hard. He thought she might be sick any moment.

"You okay?" He looked for her trash can, just in case.

She nodded weakly and swallowed again. She closed her eyes for a few moments, then cleared her throat. "Like I said before, by the time I got here, my guests were already in the conference room. So I dropped my bags by the door and went straight into the meeting. I stayed in there until the meeting ended and came to get you."

"I'll need to interview all of your coworkers to see if anyone noticed something suspicious."

"Interview us about what?" Lacy asked as she approached the cubicle.

Not knowing if Morgan had already told Lacy about the earlier roses and photos, he blocked her access to the cubicle.

"It's okay," Morgan said. "Lacy knows about the other ones."

"Other ones?" Lacy tried to look over Brady's shoulder.

He stepped back.

"Oh, roses...you mean roses. He was here, too?" Lacy slipped past Brady to squat by Morgan and take her hands. "Do you think he works here? With us?"

"Don't jump to conclusions," Brady warned. "This doesn't mean he's a coworker."

Lacy shook her head as if still not believing her eyes. "But he could be, right?"

"It's possible."

"Nantz." She dropped Morgan's hands and swiveled to look up at Brady. "It has to be Nantz."

"No." Morgan swung her head forcefully side to side then stopped to take a few deep breaths. All color had drained from her face and perspiration glistened on her forehead. Brady couldn't tell if this news was hitting her harder than last night or if she wasn't feeling well.

"Morgan?" he asked. "Are you okay?"

She blinked a few times. "Fine."

"So who is this Nantz person?" he asked.

"Our supervisor. Silas Nantz. But I think Lacy is overreacting here. I'm sure he wouldn't do something like this."

"I don't agree," Lacy said firmly. "Nantz has a crush on Morgan. It's so pitifully obvious, but he hasn't said a thing to her about it. I figure he's following work protocol and not hitting on her because he's her supervisor. He's kind of a jerk, though, and I could totally see him doing this."

"I certainly can't," Morgan said.

Brady planted his feet on the carpet. "I'll want to talk to him."

Morgan crossed her arms "You're not planning on accusing him of anything, are you? I don't want my supervisor to be embarrassed because he has a little crush on me."

"Aha, so you think he has a crush, too," Lacy said.

"Okay, fine." Morgan tightened her arms. "He does. But that doesn't make him a stalker and doesn't mean this has to make him uncomfortable."

"Don't worry, I can be subtle."

Morgan looked up at him as if she didn't believe him, and surprisingly, her opinion hurt.

She shifted her gaze to Lacy. "I didn't ask what brought you back here."

"I was just going to tell you I was leaving for lunch."

Morgan turned her focus to Brady. "Do you need to ask Lacy any questions or is she free to go?"

"Just a couple of quick things. I'm assuming by your reaction you haven't seen the roses before now, but did you see anyone in the building who seemed out of place?"

"I've been up front all morning with clients. It was just our usual group."

"Could one of them have gotten back here?"

Lacy shook her head. "They have no need to access this part of the building. They have everything they need up front, including a restroom. Even so, if we leave the resource room, we lock the adjoining door."

She offered Brady a tight smile. "I wish I could help more, but that's all I know." She stood. "I'm going to grab lunch. Can I bring anything back for you guys?"

"Depends on Morgan's schedule." Brady focused on her. "Can you take time to go to lunch?"

"Yes."

"Then thanks for the offer, but we're good."

"Don't worry, sweetie." Lacy gave Morgan's shoulder a squeeze. "Everything will work out just the way it's supposed to."

Having a good friend like Lacy was important. Brady had the same thing with his FRS teammates as friends, proving the importance of having strong relationships in his life.

Just not a relationship with a woman, huh?

Brady ignored his thoughts and watched Lacy walk away. "She seems nice."

"I wouldn't have my job without her," Morgan said enthusiastically. "I was volunteering here and we started talking. She told me about the opening." Morgan smiled, then sat forward as if resolved to move on. "So, about lunch. You want that cheeseburger you mentioned?"

He liked seeing this lighter side of her and wished she wasn't under such tension so he could get to know the real Morgan. Just the kind of thought that could get him into big trouble.

He needed to stick to the investigation. Maybe see if she even wanted him to help figure out who was stalking her. "I've kind of butted in today and didn't ask if you wanted my help investigating this."

Her smile faltered. "You're not having second thoughts, are you?"

"I'm glad to help, but, I want to make sure you'd like me to work on this."

"Yes, thank you. I'd appreciate it."

"I'll have to give Rossi a call to bring him up to speed and ask if he's amenable to my doing a little digging around in my free time." He firmly met her gaze. "One thing I've got to say first."

"Name it."

"I need you to keep an open mind about whatever I find. You'll want to avoid or refuse to believe things about the people you know, but that could put you in a very dangerous position."

"I'll do my best," she said.

Honestly, he wasn't convinced she would comply, and he had his work cut out for him in getting her to see that danger could be coming from people close to her. "I'd like to start by taking a look at your calendar for the last few months to see where you might have intersected with potential suspects so we can check them out."

"Okay."

"Also, as I mentioned, I'll want to talk with the staff here. And, of course, after Lacy's comments, I'll be conducting a thorough interview with Nantz."

She eyed him, her resolve apparent in the tilt of her head. "I'm okay with setting that up, but I don't want to alienate all my coworkers so promise me you'll be diplomatic."

"Sure," he promised, though if it came down to pressing one of these people or holding back, he'd err on the side of being pushy if it would gain him additional information. "I'd like to suggest we invite Archer to join us for lunch."

"Archer? He's the guy who tried to talk Craig down last night, right?"

Brady nodded. "He's well versed in the characteristics of stalkers, and I'd like him to share his knowledge with us. That way, as I investigate, I can watch for these traits. You'll be able to evaluate men you know in a new light, too."

"Is that really necessary?" She sounded so weary he hated to continue, but her life depended on it.

"A normal person doesn't break in and leave surprises, Morgan. Which means we're dealing with an unbalanced individual who could take this to the next level in a heartbeat."

"Meaning?"

"Meaning he might try to end your life."

Panic raced into her eyes as if she'd just realized the danger she might be in. Realized that, except for him, she was completely alone. And in that moment, he discovered just how much he hated the thought of her being so vulnerable to a dangerous attack.

Morgan adjusted her silverware, lining it up and making sure everything was perfectly spaced. Other diners and restaurant staff in the burger place were laughing while she sat there listening to Archer provide details about the man who could be stalking her. She not only didn't want to hear the details, she didn't even want to admit she had a stalker.

"Morgan." Brady leaned closer drawing her attention. "Did you hear Archer? Is there a shy man in your life who might be afraid to face you and declare his affection?"

Was there? She ran through the men she regularly interacted with and came up empty. "No."

"Maybe a client," Brady continued.

She shook her head. "I don't have that kind of relationship with my clients."

"That you know of," Archer said. "And I should point out that this guy isn't likely shy. Someone who is timid is not someone with enough nerve to break into your home."

"But you just said he could be shy," Brady argued.

"No, I said if we weren't dealing with a true stalker, he could be shy. But the break-ins suggest classic stalker mentality."

"Which is what?" Brady asked, sounding testy.

He appeared to be as frustrated as she was about figuring out who was leaving the roses. She had no idea why it bothered him so much. Beside the fact that he seemed to feel responsible for protecting her. She sensed that he found her attractive, but she also got the feeling that something about her bothered him. What, she had no idea.

Archer faced her. "Maybe it would be helpful

if I explained the three basic types of stalkers and you can think about men in your life who might fit the categories."

Helpful, yes. Uncomfortable, yes. Necessary, yes.

"Go ahead," she said, and prepared herself for what she was about to hear.

"Okay, so we have the antisocial, narcissistic and bully categories."

Morgan shivered. "Just hearing the categories makes them all sound like people I wouldn't want anywhere near me."

"Trust me, if we're dealing with a true stalker, you don't want to meet him." The gravity of Archer's tone made her cringe.

Brady's hand resting on the tablecloth tightened into a fist before he pulled out a notebook and pen from his jacket pocket.

"I'll start with a few general characteristics." Archer held up his index finger. "First, stalkers are usually above average in intelligence." Up went the next finger. "Second, they have an obsessive personality and don't display the discomfort or anxiety that people would naturally feel in many situations." Another finger shot up. "Third, they're loners and don't have a relationship outside the stalking one. And last—" he raised the fourth finger and paused for added effect. "They usually have low self-esteem, though they work hard to hide it."

Brady looked up from his note taking. "This sound like anyone you know, Morgan? Nantz, maybe?"

"I can't rule him out based on these characteristics," she said, hating the fact that she was casting suspicion on a man who—as far as she knew—hadn't acted improperly. "But, honestly, my gut still says he's not the guy. Wouldn't he have made his interest known by now?"

"Not necessarily," Archer said. "He could be testing the waters to see how you feel about his approach. And he could even be doing this to make you turn to him for help and support."

"I suppose it's possible," she admitted reluctantly.

"It would help if you told us more about each group." Brady held his pen at the ready.

Archer nodded. "So, let's start with the antisocial male. He's impulsive, reckless and can't postpone gratification. In that respect, he thinks of other people as objects he can manipulate to help him find gratification. He'd have very little conscience. No empathy. He operates outside social norms. Lies a lot. Of all the categories, this guy is the most aggressive and violent."

Brady looked at her. "This sound like Nantz?"

"Thankfully, no." She sighed out a breath of relief. "Not at all."

"Fit Preston?"

"I thought we'd ruled him out because he's out of town."

"You may have, but I didn't," Brady said. "He could have hired someone to do this."

"That's kind of far-fetched, isn't it, bro?" Archer asked.

Brady lifted his chin. "How so?"

"True stalkers don't hire others to do the work for them. They take joy and satisfaction in their actions." Archer leaned back in his chair and looked at Brady.

Morgan couldn't help but compare the two. Brady was tough and rugged looking. Archer was more refined, yet not any less powerful. He looked more like the kind of guys she'd dated. His clothes were expensive while Brady's were more practical and budget friendly. Archer would fit in with her family. Brady would stand out like a sore thumb. Despite it all, Brady was the one who made her heart beat faster—and he was also the one who made her feel safe.

She shook off her thoughts in time to hear Archer say, "If this Preston guy is stalking Morgan, then he'd most likely be leaving the roses and pictures himself."

Brady's jaw tightened. "Fine. We'll forget about Preston for now, but if anything changes, we'll reconsider him again. Let's move on to the narcissistic type."

Archer sat forward. "He feels grandiose and

self-important. He's arrogant and haughty. He's firmly convinced that he's unique and likely exaggerates his accomplishments, talents and skills. He requires excessive admiration, attention and affirmation."

As the description sank in, Morgan's heart constricted. Archer could easily be talking about Nantz. As much as she hated to admit it, she would. "This sounds more like Nantz."

"Then we have our first official suspect." Brady's eyes gleamed with satisfaction.

Morgan looked at him. "Remember you promised to go easy on all the staff when you talk to them."

"That was before I heard this. Now, I'll do whatever it takes to find out if Nantz is involved."

That's what Morgan was afraid of. "I love my job, Brady, and I don't intend to lose it because you decided to play hardball with Nantz. If you want access to him, you've got to promise to take it easy in the initial interview. Then we'll talk about what you discover and go from there."

"I'll try. Unless, of course, he confesses." Brady grinned. "That's a whole other story."

She could see how much he loved his job, and she suspected he was very good at it, but she hoped he wouldn't destroy her wonderful working environment in the process.

He turned his attention to Archer. "And the last guy? The bully."

"As you'd expect, bullies feel inadequate and compensate with violence. Not just physical, but verbal and psychological. They're a lot like the antisocial personality in that they are insincere, haughty and lack empathy. They also treat people as objects to help find gratification. But a bully differs in that he is ruthless, and blames others for his failures. He has low frustration levels and gets bored easily. These guys are immature and real control freaks. But they're more socially adept than the other categories and they can be fun to be around. You have to spend some time with them to see their dysfunctional personality."

"That's totally not Nantz," Morgan said.

Brady looked at her and held her gaze. "Archer's made it very clear that this man is in your life, Morgan. Don't miss seeing these characteristics just because you don't want to see them."

He kept staring at her, and she shrank back at his intensity. Gone was the sweet guy who'd talked of caring for a calf and was sad when it was sold. The gentle guy who held her earlier. This man staring at her was the rock-solid guy who could easily pull the trigger on his rifle.

The sight scared her as much as it made her feel safe.

"I'm sorry I sound so doom and gloom," he said. "But you don't have to worry. I won't leave you alone. I'll be with you as you go through the rest of your day."

"Make sure you don't stop at considering the men you know by name," Archer added. "The stalker may be someone you interact with or simply see on a regular basis, but don't really know."

"I see a lot of men in the course of the day."

"Exactly," Brady said gravely. "Which is why we need to look at all men within your circle. And do it quickly. After hearing these characteristics, we can't waste any time finding him."

SEVEN

In the small PEA conference room, Brady stretched and closed his notebook. He'd talked with every staff member who was in the office that morning. Including Nantz, who fit many of the narcissistic stalker traits as Morgan had said.

She poked her head into the room Brady had been using all afternoon. "That was the last person. Did anyone give you anything to go on?"

"No one saw the roses being left, if that's what you're asking. And, except for Nantz, I don't see the other men who work here fitting the stalker personality."

She moved deeper into the room. "But you still think Nantz is a possibility?"

"He has access to your cubicle, which means your keys. Obviously, he has access to this building and his cubicle is close to yours. Plus he has plenty of holes in his schedule when he could have left the roses in all three locations. So, yeah, I think he's not only a possibility, but a strong suspect."

She frowned. "So what happens next?"

"I'll start a background check on him and call Rossi to bring him into the loop." Brady closed the notebook he'd used to jot down his thoughts during the interviews. "You need to be prepared for Rossi wanting to interview workers here, too."

"That's not going to make me very popular," she said. "But it can't be helped, I suppose."

"Not if we want to find your stalker, and I know you want to do that as soon as possible."

"I just wish I could think of who might be doing this. I know you think it's Nantz, but I don't get a creeper vibe from him."

"Time will tell," Brady said. "What's up next on your schedule?"

"I have a small group of clients coming in. I'll spend my afternoon working with them."

"Any of them men?"

She nodded reluctantly. "Don't tell me you want to add them to the suspect list, too?"

"No, but I would like to see how they interact with you. Maybe I'll notice something you aren't seeing. Why don't I make that call to Rossi, then join you in the resource room?" She looked like she planned to argue the point so he held up his hand. "I promise to keep a low profile." He added a smile for good measure.

"I haven't gotten any complaints from your earlier interviews, so I guess I can trust you," she said with humor.

"Just give me time." He winked at her and quirked a wicked smile.

She laughed sincerely, her face lighting with joy—real joy he hadn't witnessed in her before. His heart gave a little twinge, surprising him and leaving him uncertain about his next move. He hadn't felt the warm sensation curling through his body for a very long time. Maybe ever. And now wasn't the time to explore it.

He quickly held up his phone and forced a professional edge to his tone. "I should get to that call with Rossi. Should only take a few minutes."

Her smile fell. "I'll see you in the resource room, then." Her shoulders settled into that hard line of determination he'd seen several times now and she marched out.

He'd have to be blind not to see that his abrupt change in attitude hurt her. He regretted that, but it couldn't be helped. It was better that he hurt her now than lead her down a path that would go nowhere.

He turned his attention to his phone and had Rossi on the line in a matter of minutes. Brady relayed their latest discovery and asked if Rossi minded his help with the investigation.

"Are you kidding?" Rossi replied. "It's not every day another officer agrees to take on a case that I can't find time for. Keep me in the loop and make sure my LT doesn't find out I let a deputy from another agency work one of my cases."

Brady assured Rossi and filled him in on the morning interviews.

"Sounds like you've got this under control," Rossi said. "I could interview the coworkers, too, if you think it will help."

Brady remembered Morgan's plea not to upset her fellow workers. "I'm confident that I learned everything we need to know—other than digging into Nantz's background, which I plan to do tonight."

"You know I'm just a phone call away if something develops, right?"

"I do," Brady replied.

"While I have you on the phone," Rossi continued, "I wanted to mention we entered the prints lifted from Morgan's house and car in AFIS."

"And?" Brady asked.

"The two sets of prints match, but we struck out with AFIS. Like I said we likely lifted the ex-fiancé's prints and he's not in the system."

Brady wasn't letting this go so easily. "Could you email the prints to me so I can compare them to Nantz's?"

"Sure, man, that I can do."

Brady gave Rossi his email address.

"Oh, and I should also mention," Rossi said. "I've been through the threat file. Four letters in all. One from our shooter, Shaw. One from a woman and two from other men. All three, on the surface, appear to be upstanding citizens, but then so does Shaw. FYI, he's been arraigned and bail was denied, as we expected."

"Good. That's one less suspect to worry about."

"I'll interview the others as soon as I can."

"Let me know what you find." Brady disconnected and started for the resource room.

In the hallway, he saw Nantz heading in the opposite direction. Brady slipped inside Nantz's cubicle and grabbed an empty cup from a fast-food place in hopes of getting Nantz's prints. Brady made another quick stop in the break area and found a plastic bag to protect the cup. After hiding it in Morgan's cubicle, he joined her in the resource room.

Seated at the table with a male that Brady put in his late fifties, her back was to him and she gave no indication that she had any idea Brady had entered the room. The man was giving a bunch of excuses for his lack of success with job hunting and Morgan seemed very willing to listen to them.

Brady thought the excuses all sounded pretty lame, but instead of getting frustrated, Morgan's sincere interest showed that she wanted to help him set up a plan to succeed. And that's what she did, delving in, asking additional questions, encouraging the man to open up and provide her with the real issues holding him back.

Brady leaned against the wall and continued to watch. She moved on to the next person, showing the same care and concern. Her heart was in her work. That was clear. She loved it. Loved helping these people. She'd bridged the gap between her upbringing and these down-on-their-luck people. She didn't judge. Didn't berate. She was the real deal. Which was well and good in her professional life, but what about her personal life? Was she still the Uptown Girl?

He imagined her accompanying him to visit his mother, who still lived in the same old trailer in the sticks of Minnesota. His mom would be wearing her favorite ratty blue sweater, in her hand a plate of the golden-brown Norwegian pancakes they'd frequently eaten because they were cheap. She'd invite Morgan to sit on the worn furniture as they crossed over the torn linoleum.

Every month, Brady sent as much of his pay as he could to his mom, but while it kept food on the table and the bills paid, it still didn't stretch to fixing up her place. Which meant it couldn't stretch to him getting married and starting a family. So he'd had to make a change in employment. He'd hated to leave the marines, where he felt equal with the men and women around him. Everyone was poorly paid. A lot of the enlisted men had less than ideal backgrounds like his. He was right at home with them. But he wanted more. A family. Kids. Which meant money, so he'd moved on to get a degree and increase his income.

And now, here he sat with Morgan, his interest in her growing when falling for her or any other woman was in direct opposition to waiting until he'd finished his degree and saved enough money to properly provide for a family. No way he'd bring up a child in a disadvantaged household like he grew up in.

Not that it mattered.

He could never see Morgan with his mother. In his world. Ever. Even if Morgan embraced helping the less fortunate, she wouldn't want to live it in her own life. He was sure of that.

Morgan stared at her plate of salmon, roasted green beans and garlic mashed potatoes. It turned her stomach just looking at the food, but with Brady watching her carefully from across the table, she had to eat. If she mentioned how nauseous she'd been feeling all day, plus the nagging headache that had developed in the last few hours, she suspected he'd insist on Darcie looking at her or worse, he'd drag her to a doctor. Neither was necessary.

Not when she knew both symptoms were from stress. Just like she'd experienced every day during the trial for the mill. Back then, she'd used exercise and long bubble baths to alleviate her symptoms, and she'd do the same thing tonight.

First, she had to force down this meal. She took a bite of potatoes and swallowed as she looked at Brady. He was taking in the room, seeming unusually uncomfortable. But why?

Morgan tried to look through his eyes at the private club with a costly membership fee and was restricted to invitation only. Rich drapes hung on the windows and thick grass cloth wallpaper covered the walls. Pricey linens and place settings sat in front of them, and expensive leather chairs circled the table.

The word *pretentious* came to mind. She didn't know Brady's background, but even with her upbringing, it was easy to see the snobbishness of her parents' club. She could see why he'd feel out of place while she felt right at home. She'd had dinner here most Friday nights as she'd grown up. Still met her mother here for lunch, which was why it was on her calendar and why Brady had wanted to check it out. Now he was looking like he wished he hadn't insisted.

As the host for this meal, it was up to her to make him feel more at ease.

"How's your steak?" she asked, to engage him in conversation.

"Perfect," he replied and sliced another bite. "You come here often?"

She shook her head and forked a few green beans. "I did growing up, but now only with my mom for lunch. My budget doesn't stretch to meals like this on my own."

"I know you said there wasn't anyone here that you could think of who might target you, but now that we're here, has anyone come to mind?'

"No, why? Are you seeing someone suspicious?"

"No. Everyone seems too caught up in their own world to even notice you exist."

"Ouch." She laughed.

"You know what I mean."

"I do. They're kind of a pretentious lot, aren't they?"

"Not something I'm used to, that's for sure." He looked down and held out the tie the maître d' had provided. "You should have warned me I had to wear a coat and tie. I own them, you know, and I wouldn't have to wear this house jacket."

"I'm sorry. I didn't even think of it. My dad and Preston don't think anything of borrowing a coat if they drop in unexpectedly."

"I doubt they were wearing five-year-old Wranglers and a T-shirt," he said, the discomfort heavy in his words.

She should have considered his attire—maybe that he hadn't shaved—but she liked the scruffy beard forming. Liked the way his jeans and T-shirt fit. She couldn't very well tell him that.

"You mentioned growing up in Minnesota," she said, changing the subject. "How'd you end up in Portland?"

"It started with the marines right out of high school. I left them about five years ago and took time to backpack across the country. You know, to get a good look at the place I'd been fighting for. County had a job opening for a sniper, and I liked how open and accepting people in Portland are. Seemed like a good fit and a good place to finish my college degree."

"How long have you lived here?"

"Four years."

"So you haven't been here long. Think you'll stay?" she asked, hating to admit she was very invested in hearing him say yes.

He shrugged. "Depends on my mother back in Minnesota. She's getting older, and it'll be hard to get her to move out here." He huffed a laugh. "Unless there are grandchildren involved and that's not happening any time soon."

No children? Her heart suddenly ached and she needed more details. "You don't want to get married and have kids?"

"Sure, but I'm not in a position to even consider that." He looked like he wanted to say something more, but started lining up the salt, pepper and sugar containers instead.

"Right now," he said, keeping his gaze on his hands, "I send most of my pay to Mom, and that doesn't leave much for a guy to support a family."

He sounded so defensive, but Morgan had no idea why. She hadn't known him long, but she did know he was an honorable man. Even more honorable if he was supporting his mother. If he didn't have much money, it surely didn't mean he was less of a man.

Unless, of course, he was like her dad, whose

self-worth was tied up in his income and status. Maybe Brady was like that. She wouldn't be surprised. A lot of men felt that way.

"What about you?" he asked, still not looking up. "Since you were engaged, I gotta assume you're planning to settle down someday."

"Maybe someday," she answered vaguely and took a bite of her salmon.

He looked up. Met her gaze. Transmitted an unspoken question about her evasive answer.

His plea didn't move her to speak. She liked him. He seemed to feel the same way, and she could honestly admit she'd like to get to know him better. But even if she wasn't trying to get her own life under control instead of starting a new relationship, they couldn't afford to let emotions distract them. They had a stalker to find.

EIGHT

Brady turned in the awful tie and jacket and stepped outside with Morgan. He handed his parking ticket to the valet and couldn't wait to get out of here. He'd told Morgan the truth. He owned a suit and tie. He just didn't mention that the only time he'd worn it in the last few years was to Skyler and Logan's wedding, and only then because the entire team made up the wedding party.

The valet pulled up in Brady's rusted-out pickup. He smirked as he gestured for Brady to take charge of the vehicle. Brady ignored the guy's attitude and handed him a generous tip. Brady opened the door for Morgan, who either didn't notice the valet or was good at hiding what she witnessed. Brady suspected she was embarrassed to arrive in his battered truck when top-dollar cars surrounded them and filled the lot. Honestly, he was embarrassed, too. He was thirty-one years old, for crying out loud. He should have his act together and have a decent vehicle by now.

Patience, he reminded himself as he fired up the truck and took off. Two more years of college and he'd have his degree. Then he'd be able to drive Morgan around in style. Ha! Like he'd be in her life in two years.

He pointed the truck toward the firehouse where he'd grab workout clothes for a visit to Morgan's gym. At least he'd be more comfortable there than in her fancy club.

She was an enigma. She was so natural and in her element working with her clients. Then she took him to her exclusive club, and there, too, she fit right in.

Which woman was she, anyway? And how was a guy to know?

He glanced at her, surprised to see her massaging her forehead. "Headache?"

"A little one."

Concern for her sent his frustration packing. "Maybe we shouldn't go to the gym."

She shook her head. "It's just stress. Exercise might help."

They continued toward the firehouse in silence. He parked in front and grabbed the bag containing Nantz's cup.

Morgan leaned toward the front window. "You all live here, huh?"

"Amazing, right?" he said, looking at the impressive historic building through her eyes. "A woman—Winnie Kerr—was grateful to Darcie for saving her life, so she donated the place to County for FRS members. We all share the first floor, but we each have a private condo on the second and third floors. And we don't pay a cent in rent or for utilities. Everything's covered by an endowment fund." He smiled. "You'll get a better idea of what I mean when we go in."

Together they exited the truck and stepped toward the brick house decorated with twinkling white lights strung from every spot possible.

"Good thing you all don't have to pay the power bill for all of these lights."

He chuckled. "It's Skyler. She's really into the whole Christmas thing."

Morgan looked up at him. "Sounds like you're not."

"It was never a big deal in my family growing up," he said without further explanation, and opened the door to reveal additional decorations in the foyer.

An industrial staircase led to their condos and showcased a banner that was strung with garland and lights. Poinsettias sat on the steps and a small tree filled the corner of the entry. He led Morgan into the family room, a wide-open space where fire trucks used to park. The FRS worked out of the sheriff's office, but Winnie built a special garage across the driveway for their truck so if they weren't on duty, they wouldn't have to report to the office for a callout.

His teammates' voices echoed under the first floor's high ceilings that carried ductwork and pipes across the space.

"Wow," Morgan said as she turned, her eyes wide with wonder. "Even without all the amazing decorations, this place is so cool. I especially like that you kept the big red fire doors and it still feels like an old firehouse."

"All Winnie's doing. She remodeled the whole place with our team in mind."

"Can I see the rest of the place?"

"Sure. Sounds like the team's in the dining room. I'll have someone take you on a tour while I grab my clothes." He led the way to the dining area that was big enough for the team and guests. Brady stopped in the doorway to wait for the conversation to die down so he could properly introduce Morgan.

All team members were present except Skyler. Cash's fiancée, Krista, had joined them, too. Her grandfather, Otto, often accompanied her to dinner, but he was absent tonight. Krista and Cash had been engaged for six months now, and were hinting at a spring wedding. Cash had already asked Brady to be his best man.

They'd finished eating but were still too busy talking to notice Brady's arrival.

"I see it was Cash's night to cook," Brady said loudly to gain their attention, and then pointed at the bucket of takeout fried chicken.

"I'm working on teaching him," Krista said, and winked at Cash. "But honestly, he's hopeless."

Morgan eased past Brady and all eyes went to her, his team quickly sizing her up. Deputies made split-second decisions all the time on the job and that meant making quick determinations about people. Darcie, of course, knew Morgan, Archer had spent lunchtime with them, and the others had seen her at the standoff. If they'd already formed an opinion of her, no one had mentioned it. For a reason Brady wasn't about to dig into, he cared what they thought about her. Cared too much about it for his own good.

"You all remember Morgan," he said, and quickly brought the team up to date on her stalker situation.

Jake frowned from his seat at the end of the table. "You don't think it's related to the standoff on the train, do you?"

"I'm pretty sure it's just coincidental timing." Brady held up his hand. "And before you guys say you don't believe in coincidences, this is one of those times."

"Wait." Darcie set down one of her knitting projects for foster kids and came to her feet. "You're telling me that the break-in at Morgan's apartment happened last night and it's the first I'm hearing about it?"

"Ah, yeah," Brady said. "Sorry."

She turned to Jake. "And you knew about it, too?"

He nodded.

"Seriously." She fired a pointed look at Jake, then turned to thump Brady in the biceps. "You guys really have to do a better job of communicating."

"Hey," Cash grumbled. "I didn't know a thing about it so don't lump me in with them."

"That's because you haven't thought about anything other than Krista in months," Archer said.

Cash grinned, not at all embarrassed about his obvious devotion to Krista. "Can't think of a better way to stay out of the doghouse with Darcie than this." He tightened his arm around Krista's shoulders, and she blushed bright red.

Darcie faced Archer. "And you? Did you know?"

He nodded, but looked at Morgan. "Anything more I can do to help with the investigation?"

"We're good," Brady replied. "I'm still processing all the details you gave us about stalkers at lunch. More would just be overload."

"But we appreciate your help," Morgan added. "I think it was just what we needed to find whoever's leaving the roses and messages."

Cash removed his arm from Krista and leaned forward, the peaceful expression gone, his gaze fixed on Brady. "You need anything other than Archer's psychobabble, you know I'm your guy, right?"

"Hey, man." Archer mocked a glare. "Sometimes that so-called psychobabble is more important that all your beefy muscles."

Cash's mouth dropped open. "Beefy? I'm not beefy."

"Actually." Krista laid a hand on his shoulder. "You are kind of beefy. In a good way, though. A very good way," she added, and another blush crept over her face.

Cash smiled at her and they seemed to forget all about the others in the room.

Archer cleared his throat. "This is not what I was going for with my insult."

"Sorry, man. I'm as happy to rise to a good insult as the next guy." Cash leaned back, took Krista's hand and lifted it. "But you're gonna have to time them for when Krista's not around. She takes all the fight out of me."

Jake stuck a finger in his mouth and faked a gag.

Smiling, Morgan asked, "Are they always like this?"

"Pretty much," Brady said. "Except when we're on a callout. Things get tense there so we like to let go when we're not on duty."

"About that help." Jake brought them back to the point as he always did. "What do you need?"

"Right now, for someone to give Morgan a quick tour of the first floor while I grab some workout clothes. Morgan and I are going to check out her gym."

"I'll do it." Darcie stepped forward. "I need to catch up with Morgan anyway and make sure she has my number so she'll *call me* next time she's in trouble." Darcie's pointed look moved to Morgan, and she linked arms with her. "You *will* call me, right?"

A sheepish expression on her face, Morgan nodded. Then she glanced back at Brady as Darcie led her from the room, but he couldn't tell if she was asking to be rescued or if she was glad to be going with Darcie.

He stepped over to Jake. "Could I get you to run some prints for me?"

"A stalker suspect?"

"Loosely."

Jake's eyebrows rose. "Isn't Rossi taking care of this?"

"He's officially working the case, but with little to go on, it's not a top priority for him so I'm helping out in my spare time."

"Want me to talk to his supervisor?"

Brady shook his head. "He's got a big caseload, and we can help him out by running these, right? If they match the prints lifted at Morgan's house and her car, I'll let Rossi know."

Jake took the cup. "I'll take care of it."

"I'll email you the prints lifted at Morgan's place so our tech can compare them." Brady turned to leave, then stopped. "I'll need that ASAP."

Jake shook his head. "Of course you will."

"Hey." Brady grinned. "You've got clout. If anyone can make it happen fast, it's you."

To Jake's groan, Brady headed up the flight of metal stairs to his one-bedroom condo. He'd moved in four years ago and it didn't look much different from the day he'd first stepped in the door. Except maybe the sixty-inch TV he'd splurged on and his clothes tossed all over the furniture. Today would have been laundry day and he had to admit the place looked like a teen-age boy lived there. Hadn't taken him long to let go of regimented marine standards when it came to his personal space. Standards regarding shoot-ing hadn't changed one bit. *If* he managed to pull the trigger.

He quickly picked things up in case Darcie brought Morgan upstairs, then shoved clean work-out clothes into a bag and jogged downstairs.

He heard Darcie's voice coming from the game room. "You quit your career because of one case?"

Brady wanted to hear Morgan's answer so he joined them.

"Sounds like that, doesn't it?" Morgan replied as she glanced at him, then returned her focus to Darcie. "But actually, when things got ugly in the trial, I turned to my faith to find some peace and I left because of that."

"Really?" Darcie asked, looking up from another knitting project. She left them all over the house so whenever she had a free moment she could knit a few rows. "I never got the feeling in college that you were into your faith."

"I wasn't."

"What changed?" Brady inserted himself in the conversation and leaned against the doorjamb.

Morgan turned her attention to him and didn't seem to mind him butting in. "I was raised in the church. We went every Sunday because it was expected of our family. We didn't live our faith. It was just another thing we did to keep up our image in the community. But then came the trial." A long sigh slipped out. "It was hard seeing the suffering the plaintiffs lived with every day. I wanted to help them, but my job was to do just the opposite."

Darcie set down her needle and squeezed Morgan's hand. "With your save-the-world personality that must have been hard."

"You have no idea." The agony she'd experienced hung in her words.

"And this led you to rely on God more?" Brady asked.

She nodded. "I was headed toward a breakdown." She twisted her hands together. "Honestly, I thought I was going to completely fall apart, but there was this man who caught my attention. He'd lost his wife and two children to cancer, but he wasn't bitter like the others. He wanted a settlement because he wanted our company to take responsibility, but he didn't seem to hate us. So I started watching him to see why he was different and learned he relied on God. I figured if this guy could give it a go, so could I. I went to church one Sunday and slowly but surely discovered the value of faith in my everyday life."

Brady could tell she was about to say something more, but she stopped.

"And?" Darcie asked before Brady could.

"And, as I grew in my faith, I knew I needed to simplify my life. I was done with the whole power struggle and lifestyle that came with the kind of money my parents have. I decided to find a job where I could put my faith into action and get away from my parents' superficial world. I'd worked for my dad since graduating law school and lived in the family guesthouse. It was time to build a life for myself. I resigned, took the director's position at PEA and moved out of the guesthouse. Here I am. A much happier person. Minus the stalker, of course." She laughed.

"Wow." Darcie fell back in her chair. "You've really changed."

"For the better, I hope."

"Actually, I never saw any bad in you before,

but I'm impressed with the way you've committed your life to helping others."

"So am I," Brady said.

She looked first at Brady, then Darcie. "I get
that this isn't news to you. All of you put your
lives on the line for others every day. You're living
your faith, too." She glanced at Brady. "I guess I
shouldn't assume you're a man of faith."

"He is," Darcie said before he could speak.
"Everyone on the team is. It's a wonderful environment to work in."

Morgan peered at Darcie. "Does that have
something to do with why you changed jobs?"

"Ah, now, who said we were talking about me
today?" Darcie gathered up her bright yellow yarn
and stood. "That's a story that'll take far more
time than you two have right now."

"Then we'll make the time to catch up, okay?"

"Sure," Darcie replied, but Brady knew it was
halfhearted. Darcie didn't talk with just anyone
about the loss of her daughter or her husband
walking out on her. He wasn't sure he or anyone
on the team knew the full story.

"So," he said to Morgan, "did you get the full
VIP tour or is there still more to see?"

"She's seen everything on the first floor," Darcie replied. "And she sure doesn't want to see your
messy old condo."

"It's not that bad."

"Right." Darcie laughed and rolled her eyes,

then suddenly sobered. "Keep an eye on Morgan, okay? She's got a headache, and I don't want her to overdo it at the gym."

Brady turned to Morgan. "You work fast. Fifteen minutes at the house and Darcie's already mothering you like she does the rest of us."

Darcie smiled sincerely. "I wouldn't have to be the mother if you guys didn't think you were invincible."

Brady held up his hands. "Hey, don't unmask us in front of Morgan. She still thinks we've got superpowers."

Darcie punched Brady's shoulder. "Get out of here before I tell her exactly what you're like."

Laughing, Morgan and Brady went to the truck. Once on the road, Morgan swiveled toward him. "I like your friends. They're quite a group."

He nodded his agreement. "Lacy seems like a good friend, too."

"She is." Morgan frowned. "I'm glad to have one good friend in my life."

"Only one?" He looked at her. "You seem like the kind of person everyone would like to be friends with."

She crossed her arms as if defending herself. "Leaving my old life behind meant leaving my old friends with it."

"West Linn isn't that far away, is it?"

"It wasn't the distance so much as it was my change in lifestyle. I can't afford to do the things my old friends like to do, and they don't much enjoy the things I can afford. Not that I'm complaining about my life. I don't need more than I have." She fell silent and stared out the window.

Brady wanted to point out that true friends didn't abandon you that easily, but he suspected she already knew that, so he kept his big mouth shut for once and focused his attention on keeping her safe.

NINE

Morgan joined Brady in the gym near the stationary bikes. She'd changed into shorts and a top that fit like a glove, displaying her toned body. She was clearly in great shape, and he appreciated her dedication to fitness. From the number of men he caught staring at her, it seemed like the other guys there did, too. He didn't like them staring at her. Not one bit.

He crossed the room toward her, catching snippets of conversations on the way. Stock trades. Public offerings. Company mergers. Medical diagnoses. Even here, he was surrounded by professionals in high-paying jobs. He wasn't surprised, but he did wonder how, if Morgan had truly left her family behind, she could afford this place. Or her apartment, for that matter.

She couldn't make much money working for a nonprofit. Did her parents still pay her membership here and at the club as well as her rent? His impression of her said she wouldn't allow that, but what else was he to think? She still seemed to be living the good life, which took money that she'd just said she didn't need.

"So what's the plan?" she asked, lacking the confidence he'd come to associate with her.

"Just do what you normally do, and I'll hang back to watch."

"Hang back?" She suddenly grinned. "Afraid I can run circles around you?"

"You want to compete?" The thought that she might be able to outdo him shocked him. "I'm game. Let's start with a little spinning." He didn't wait for a response but headed for the stationary bikes. He soon figured out the controls and started his legs pumping. "What do you say? An hour to start or is ninety minutes better?"

Her mouth dropped open, and he laughed so hard his side hurt. Man, he wished she was from his side of the tracks. He was starting to really like having her around.

She climbed on the bike next to his, and as they both pedaled away, he enjoyed finally having something in common with her. But he wouldn't let that distract him. He was here for one reason only so he kept running his gaze over the place.

A guy who was hulking and thickly muscled kept glancing at Morgan. She seemed oblivious to him as she pedaled and took sips of another one of her energy drinks.

"Don't make this obvious, but take a look at the guy on the elliptical trainer. He's been checking you out. Do you know him?"

She gradually swung her gaze in that direction, then wrinkled her nose. "Kurt? Kurt Eckert. He's asked me out more times than I can count, but he's not really my type so I've always turned him down."

"And how does he react?"

"He blows it off—makes a joke, but I can still see it bothers him."

A perfect reason to start stalking someone. "He fit any of our stalker profiles?"

She raised her head as if thinking, then looked at Eckert. "Yeah, maybe the bully. At first, I thought he was great, but then I spent more time around him and discovered he's really out for himself. And I once saw him berating a staff member for no good reason. I thought he might hit the poor guy."

"Suspect number two," Brady said with a smile.

She swung her gaze to Brady. "You think that makes him a suspect?"

"He's in your circle. You've turned him down. He doesn't like it. He has stalker tendencies."

"Is that really enough to consider him a suspect?"

"I don't know," Brady said, keeping a careful eye on Eckert. "But I aim to find out."

* * *

Brady grumbled under his breath before sliding into his truck next to Morgan. After a morning of investigating Eckert while Morgan worked a job fair for PEA, Brady hoped to have uncovered more than the fact that Eckert didn't have a criminal record and the guy owned what seemed to be a legit auto repair shop.

He'd expected Morgan to be upset when he'd told her he'd struck out, but she'd been preoccupied all day and it didn't seem to register. She didn't even pay much attention to Preston when he approached her table at the Expo Center. He was recruiting at the job fair and felt a need to stop by. Brady was glad to finally meet Morgan's ex, but took an instant dislike to the guy. Likely more because he'd once been engaged to Morgan and he oozed entitlement than because he was a potential stalker. She, on the other hand, had been cordial, as had Preston.

Preston. A guy wearing a designer suit and pricey shoes. He probably drove a Beemer, too. Or Lexus. Now here Morgan sat in Brady's truck where the heat didn't always work. Talk about a contrast.

He flipped on the switch and thankfully, the blower sent out warm air. Morgan dug out one of her drinks from an insulated cooler. He'd much rather have something hot, like cocoa, but she claimed her drinks gave her energy. He respected her choice to eat healthy, but what was wrong with a little sugar once in a while?

She sighed and settled back into her seat as he merged onto the road.

"Want to tell me what's been going on with you today?" He gave her a pointed look.

"Want to? No."

"But you will," he said more demanding than he should have been, but he needed to know what was up with her if he was going to protect her.

"I've got a headache. A little nausea."

"It's been bothering you all day, right?"

She nodded.

"You sure it's a good idea to go to the gym tonight?"

She held up the bottle. "This should help bring me back to life."

He would have continued to argue the point, but his phone chimed a text from Jake. At the next stoplight, he grabbed it from the dash and read the message.

"Text is from Jake. Nantz's prints are back. They don't match the ones found at your apartment or in your car."

"Can't say I'm surprised. I honestly didn't think they would."

Brady glanced at her. "You know this doesn't rule him out, right? The prints that were lifted might not be related to the break-ins at all, and Nantz could have worn gloves."

"Again, I doubt it, but I know he remains a suspect." She sighed.

He didn't know if it was because she didn't want to consider Nantz a suspect or because she was tired. "I'll try to get Eckert's prints at the gym, too. Plus, I want you to interact with him. Try to learn his whereabouts when the roses and other items were left."

"Which means I have to be nice to the guy." She mocked a shiver. "If he asks me out again, you're going to have to rescue me."

"I'll keep an eye on you. If necessary, I can pretend I'm your boyfriend."

"We'll need a signal, then. Like spies use on TV." A cute grin brightened her face as if she found the idea of an undercover mission fun. "How about I take the clip out of my hair?"

"Sounds good," Brady said and concentrated on possible scenarios he might encounter with Eckert.

When they actually met up with the guy, he was standoffish and terse. Brady expected Morgan to give up on talking to him, but instead she started flirting. Putting her hand on his arm. Batting long, long lashes up at him.

It's all an act, Brady kept reminding himself. An act Eckert obviously bought. He smiled and stepped closer, eliminating the personal space

Brady instructed Morgan to maintain. Eckert started touching Morgan's arm when he spoke. Her shoulder. Leaning even closer. Whispering.

Mine. The word shot through Brady's brain and he immediately pushed it away. She wasn't his. He didn't even want her to be his, did he?

Morgan suddenly stepped back and jerked out her hair clip. Brady charged across the room. He put an arm around her shoulders and drew her closer for protection. "Ready to go, honey?"

She smiled up at him, sincere relief shining in her eyes. Her obvious joy at seeing him sent a surge of warmth through his body and made him want it. Much more. This was exactly how it would feel if they were together. The ache for such a relationship was palpable and regret surged over not being able to act on it. She rested her hand on his chest, an expensive ruby ring on her finger bringing him back to reality. She was used to the finer things in life. Things he couldn't provide until he got his degree and had a better paying job. He'd stay his course and not risk hurting her when there was no place in his life for a relationship right now.

She looked at Eckert. "This is my boyfriend, Brady. He might be joining the gym, too."

Eckert scowled at her, his eyes filled with fury. "Then what was with all the flirting?"

"Flirting?" she asked innocently.

"Look, lady, I'm not someone you can play with and get away with it." He grabbed for her arm.

Brady stepped forward, pulling Morgan out of Eckert's reach and blocking the man's access to her.

"If you ever—" Eckert's voice rose and his face reddened as he fired a threatening look at Morgan "—ever, lead me on like that again, you'll pay. Got that, lady?"

He marched away, his strides swift and angry. A man passing by gawked at Eckert.

"What are you looking at?" Eckert barreled into the other guy, knocking him to the floor.

Morgan trembled under Brady's arm. "I'm glad you were here."

"I won't let anything happen to you, honey. Ever." He resisted the urge to charge after Eckert to teach him a few manners and hugged Morgan close. "C'mon, let's get out of here."

On the way out, Brady grabbed Eckert's disposable water bottle for prints and escorted Morgan to the locker room. Brady hated letting her out of his sight for a minute. Eckert was volatile. Out of control and a foe to be reckoned with. A man who clearly possessed stalking characteristics, making him the perfect suspect.

Morgan leaned closer to the door in Brady's truck and clutched her stomach. After her altercation with Eckert, her stomach continued to heave and roil. The bumpy ride didn't help and she could tell that throwing up was imminent.

"Can you pull over?" she asked. "Quickly. I think I'm going to be sick."

Brady swung the truck to the side of the road.

She pushed her door open and hung her head. The freezing air helped stem the nausea, but her stomach still churned. Brady came around the front of the truck and squatted in front of her. He gently moved her hair from her face and looked up at her with concern darkening his eyes.

"I wouldn't squat there if I were you," she said trying to make light of the embarrassing moment. "You're in the tsunami zone."

He chuckled, then immediately sobered. "You haven't been feeling well for days. Maybe we should have Darcie come check you out."

Morgan started to shake her head, but the world spun and she stopped. "It's just stress. It was like this during the trial, too."

"Must have been hard to win the case when you were barfing on the judge's feet."

She gave him a wan smile. "It never got this bad. I think Eckert's threats really brought things home tonight."

"Maybe you've developed an ulcer or something. Darcie could help."

"I don't need to see Darcie. I just want to go home."

"You okay for me to drive, then?"

"Yes," she said and laid her head back on the seat.

He got back in and merged into traffic. Each bump, each stop, sent her stomach churning, but she swallowed hard and willed her stomach to behave.

Thankfully, he found a spot near her building and parked. "I want to check out your apartment before you go inside."

"You think someone's been here again?"

"I have no reason to think so, but it's better to be safe than sorry." He didn't sound like he believed his own words, making her more anxious.

He reached out as if to take her hand, then let his arm drop. "I don't want to leave you out here. Can you make it inside and wait for me in the lobby?"

"Yes," she said. "Just be quick.

She let him help her up the steps and over to a seat before he boarded the elevator and disappeared. She'd never admit it to anyone, but she liked leaning on him. Liked having him want to care for her like this.

Where had all her independence gone?

The room suddenly spun and her stomach clenched. She leaned her head back on the richly covered wing-back chair and waited for the moment to pass. Maybe he'd been right. Maybe this was more that stress. Maybe she had a virus. There was one going around. Several of her clients' children had been sick.

Please, Father. I don't need to be sick, too.

The sound of the old elevator descending to the ground floor brought Morgan's head up. Thinking Brady was on his way down, she sat up to hide her wooziness before he arrived and insisted on bringing Darcie over. She sure hoped he didn't find anything in her apartment, as she just wanted to sink into her bed and go to sleep.

He stepped out of the elevator. His gaze went straight to her. His eyes and jaw were tight.

Her heart plummeted.

He didn't have to say a word. His expression said it all. Something terrible awaited her upstairs.

TEN

Morgan stood in her doorway, staring at a trail of rose petals leading down the hallway like a trail of blood. Their sweet scent, a smell she'd once loved, was cloying. She felt her stomach lurch again, and she swallowed back the urge to hurl on her wood floors.

"Remember," Brady said from right behind her. "Don't touch anything. Rossi will want to see the scene just as we found it."

She followed the trail inside. Though Brady had told her what to expect, she gasped and jerked back from the red votive candles in small glass holders burning on almost every surface in her living room. They'd obviously been lit for some time as many of the wicks had been swallowed by melted wax that extinguished the flame. On the sofa sat a large poster board covered with photographs. Photos of her engaging in her daily activities. At work in the resource room. On the MAX.

At the theater. The gym. The grocery store. Pharmacy. On and on. Her every movement.

Her stalker had been close to her. So close. All this time.

She shivered and couldn't stem the tears that had been threatening for days.

"Aw, honey, it'll be okay." Brady gently tipped her head up and looked into her eyes. "I promise."

She saw compassion, caring and warmth in his gaze and didn't want to look away. To move away.

He swiped a thumb over her cheek and despite knowing she should take a step back, she rested her forehead on the solid wall of his chest and felt herself relax. He drew her closer. Pressed her cheek against his chest and stroked her hair while she cried.

"Shh," he whispered. "I'm here, and I'm not going anywhere."

She didn't know how long she let him hold her, but the sound of Rossi calling out from the open door brought her to her senses and she backed away. Brady's eyes narrowed as if she'd hurt him. If she had, she regretted it, but despite the urge to lean on him, she couldn't do so. Not for more than a moment. Not now when she'd just begun to taste life on her own.

She dragged her gaze away from him. He went to greet Rossi in the hallway where she heard Brady bring the detective up to speed, but the collage beckoned her to take a closer look instead of joining them. Her stomach convulsing once again, she studied the pictures and tried to recall the dates of the activities. Just how long had she been watched?

She heard Brady and Rossi enter the room, then a swift indrawn gasp of air, probably from Rossi. If a hardened detective thought the collage was gasp worthy, she should be even more concerned.

"He's been following me for months," she muttered. "Three months, to be exact."

Rossi moved next to her. "How do you know?"

She pointed at a photo where she stood outside the Keller Auditorium. "This production was in October."

Frowning, Rossi moved closer to the collage. "Can you identify the timing of any of the other pictures?"

"Yes."

"Then I need you to write down the date for each picture you can match."

She peered at him, the throbbing in her head intensifying. "It sounds like you believe me now."

"I apologize for ever doubting you," he said sincerely. "But the evidence just didn't support your claim until now."

"Now?" she asked. "I'm surprised you didn't think I set this up before I left for work this morning."

"It's the candles." Brady gestured around the

room. "You've been with me all day. There's no way you could have lit these."

"Oh…right," she managed to say. She should be glad that Rossi now believed her, but the thought of a man spending all that time lighting these candles in her apartment sent terror to her heart, and she felt like she might drop to the floor.

"I suppose you could have arranged for someone to do this for you," Rossi continued. "But I'm more inclined to think you're telling the truth." Rossi met her gaze, his assessing for a moment. "I'm going to bring in forensics for this. I'll just step outside to call them, and then we'll go through the crime scene together."

Morgan settled in a chair and waited until he left the room before looking at Brady. "Why is he so suspicious?"

"He's in law enforcement. We're all suspicious." Brady grimaced. "If you saw what we do on a daily basis, you'd understand."

"What exactly do you do every day?" she asked, trying to think about anything other than the evidence of a stalker surrounding her. "I mean you can't be called out to hostage situations with the FRS all the time."

"Actually, I wear three hats." He leaned against the wall. "In addition to the FRS, I'm on the sheriff's Search and Rescue Squad. When I'm not dispatched for either of these teams, I work patrol. Since the county can't afford for the FRS to sit around and wait for a callout, everyone on the team but Jake has a secondary assignment."

"Do you like being a deputy?"

Brady hesitated. "It can be the best job in the world and the worst, but yeah, I like it."

She looked up at him, this man who was so different from the men she'd known in her sheltered life. He was earnest and hardworking. Kind. Compassionate. Smart and funny. The kind of guy a woman could settle down with and be happy. Truly happy.

"Is something wrong?" Brady pushed off the wall and took a step closer. "I mean, other than the obvious problems surrounding you?"

"Wrong? No."

"Your stomach isn't bothering you?"

"Oddly enough, it's a little better."

"Really? This situation had to take you to the top of the stress meter, so maybe it's not stress after all."

"Maybe." She suspected feeling better had more to do with Brady's strong embrace than anything, but she wouldn't tell him that.

He nodded at the collage. "Why don't you get started on that list for Rossi while I take pictures of the collage?"

"Pictures? Why?"

"Rossi will take the board as evidence. If we want to find this creep, we'll need to study the photos to see if there's a pattern."

Right. Study pictures of her taken by a crazy man. Just what she wanted to do, but it couldn't be helped. Not if they were going to put an end to this reign of terror.

She grabbed a notebook from her small desk in the corner of the room and returned to the chair. She forced herself to review the board, picture by picture, and note any dates she could remember. With the use of the calendar on her phone, she located exact dates for ten events and jotted them down. That still left twenty pictures without any precise date information, though she still listed locations when she could.

"Let me snap a photo of your list, too." Brady took it from her hands.

"Forensics is on the way," Rossi said stepping up to them. "FYI, I'm not sure if you noticed, but there's no sign of forced entry."

"That's even more significant this time, with the locks changed." Brady looked at Morgan. "Did you leave your keys unattended since we talked about it?"

"Nowhere unsecured."

"Which means what, exactly?"

"In the gym they were in my locker. At work and at the job fair, they were in my purse. So no, they weren't anywhere anyone could get to them."

"Then we're looking at someone who's skilled at picking locks." Rossi frowned. "Not a skill that a run-of-the-mill guy possesses."

"And not a skill the people I know would possess," Morgan said vehemently.

"People hide things all the time." Brady leveled a long stare at her. "Between our suspects Nantz and Eckert, I'd have to choose Eckert. His mechanical background seems more logical for someone who learned how to pick locks."

"We just don't have enough information to know," Rossi said. "Now, about the collage. Did you finish the list for me?"

Morgan handed it to him.

"I took photos of the collage so we can continue to study it," Brady said. "If we figure out any other locations or dates, we'll get the information to you."

"Good." Rossi's focus drifted to the door where footsteps sounded outside. "That will be our forensics tech. I need to give him instructions."

"Before you go," Brady said, "I grabbed a water bottle with Eckert's prints, and I can either have my team run it like they did with Nantz's prints or give it to you."

"I'll take it and rush the processing."

"It's in my car."

"No hurry. Just grab it before I take off." Rossi offered a rare smile. "You should know, I've talked to two of the four people who sent the threatening letters. Both of them have alibis and of course, Shaw was in jail. I'll get to the other guy ASAP."

He started to walk away, stopped and turned back to look at Morgan.

She didn't like the way his gaze had intensified and prepared herself for bad news.

"The DA will be contacting you about testifying at Shaw's trial," he said. "I'm assuming you're willing to do so."

Thoughts of seeing Craig Shaw again sent her pulse racing but she nodded.

"Okay, good. I'm glad we can count on you."

A tall forensic tech wearing a white Tyvek suit stepped into the room. He carried a large case and he looked focused and determined, giving Morgan some comfort that they might find evidence this time.

"Excuse me," Rossi said, and went to join him.

Brady held up his phone. "Since Rossi is still here, I'd like to run out to a copy place and have large prints of the photos made so we can get a better look at them."

"Okay." She might have agreed, but she honestly didn't want Brady to leave. She was starting to depend on him and it bothered her. Bothered her even more that she was wondering what it was going to be like after this was over and Brady went back to his life and she resumed her daily routine.

He smiled tightly. "Why don't you try to rest until I come back?"

Rest, right. Like she'd ever rest well in this

apartment, this place where she'd established her independence, ever again.

Brady had been studying the photos propped on Morgan's dining table with no success. He rearranged them, hoping to spark a new insight. Stepping back, he stared at them while trying to ignore the lingering scent of roses. After the forensic tech had finished processing the place, Morgan cleaned up the petals and Brady took out the trash, but the whole place still had a sickly sweet smell. He never wanted to see or smell a rose again, and he suspected Morgan felt the same way.

She sat at the table rubbing her forehead. At least her nausea seemed to have passed—or she was doing a better job of hiding it. She should rest, but they needed to work on the photos more. Her safety depended on it.

And it also depended on him not leaving her here alone. "I'm going to bunk on your couch at night until we find this guy."

"That's not necessary," she said, but she actually looked relieved.

"I think it is and it's not negotiable," he said firmly, and pointed at the photos to move on. "Are you up for going through the pictures one more time before we call it a night?"

She stopped massaging her head and nodded.

He started with a picture taken of her at work in the resource room. "The stalker had to have been close for this one. The angle would have precluded the use of a telephoto lens. Is there anything in the picture that could help give us a date?"

She stared at it. Turned it. Tapped it against the table, then suddenly looked up. "My suit. My dad ruined it when he spilled a glass of wine on it. I never wore it after that." She looked through her calendar program on her phone, then pointed at the screen. "Here. The dinner was on November twentieth. I was heading there right after work. That was the only time I wore that suit to the office."

"Okay, write that one down." He waited for her to finish noting the date on the list. "Anything odd or unusual about that night?"

She seemed to shrink as he asked the question. "It's the last time I had dinner alone with my father. It was his last-ditch effort to get me to come back to the mill and get back together with Preston. I refused both, and he was livid. He's kind of disowned me."

"Seems extreme."

"Self-preservation, I guess." She twined her fingers together and stared at them. "I never had any interest in running the company, and he hated to think it wouldn't be in the family after he retired. He wanted to merge the mill with Orion Transport and have Preston run the new company. The mill would stay in the family, and Dad could boss Preston around."

She slumped in her chair as sadness and a hint

of hopelessness seemed to take over. Seeing this contradiction to her usual determination broke Brady's heart. He took the chair next to her and resisted reaching for her hands. "That must have been a difficult night."

"Actually," she said, her voice low and tortured. "It got even worse. He told me I wasn't strong enough to make it on my own, that I'd come crawling back to him, back to Preston, and beg them to take me back."

"I'm sorry, Morgan." He took her hands in his, and the icy coldness confirmed her angst. "That must be hard for you."

She watched him for a moment, then suddenly freed her hands, pulled her shoulders back and let her iron curtain of resolve mask her feelings. "With my focus on achieving my professional goals, he'll see that he was wrong in due time."

Wondering if this night was significant in the stalking incidents, Brady forced his eyes over the line of photos one more time. Only one thing jumped out at him. "I guess this explains why most of these pictures are related to your job."

"Yeah, it's pretty much my whole life right now." A nervous laugh slipped out. "What am I saying? It *is* my whole life."

"And what about friends and fun?"

She looked up at him in surprise. "I love what I do, so I honestly haven't thought about it. But now that you mention it?" She shrugged. "Once

I get my life on track, I'll make time for other things and people."

"So, no time for a relationship or family?" he asked, and wondered as soon as the words left his mouth why he would ask such a question.

She shrugged again. "I'm young. That will change. I'll find someone who shares my interests and then start a family."

Right, shared interests. That ruled Brady out now and in the future.

He tapped the next photo. "Anything in this one that grabs you?"

She shook her head, and they continued through the stack, putting additional dates and details on paper.

He ran his finger down the completed list. "No pattern, really. Some are daytime, some night. Even the daytime events are spread out. What about weekday versus weekend?"

"A mix there, too."

Brady stood back. "Then either this guy works at your office, works a flexible job or is unemployed. The number of pictures taken at the office would seem to point to Nantz, but Eckert owns his business and sets his own schedule, so this doesn't rule either of them out." Brady dug out his phone. "I'll text the additional information to Rossi. Maybe he'll see something in the pattern."

While Brady sent the text, Morgan gathered the pictures and put them away. He didn't blame her for not wanting to leave them displayed. He wasn't the intended target and they still creeped him out. He couldn't imagine how she was feeling.

He stowed his phone and looked at the clock, the hands nearing midnight. "We should try to get some sleep." He glanced at the tiny sofa, his body already aching from the thought of trying to sleep on it.

"You're not going to fit on it, are you?" she asked, the weakest of smiles breaking free.

"You know I won't. That's why you're smiling. Imagining my big feet flopping over the end," he continued, hoping to see her smile grow.

"Sorry. I don't mean to find humor in your discomfort, but…" She grinned up at him in earnest now.

Her smile caught him unaware, tugging at his heart. He looked away before he did something stupid like try to kiss her. "Sorry to disappoint you, but I'll just bunk on the floor. I've done it enough times in the marines. No biggie."

"I'll get blankets and a pillow." She stood and looked like she was going to keel over. She grabbed the table.

He reached for her elbow and settled her onto the chair again. She blinked a few times, her long lashes batting quickly, a vacant stare on her face.

He squatted in front of her. "Morgan. Are you okay?"

"Just a little dizzy. It's been a stressful night."

The fade of adrenaline could cause her symptoms, but he didn't want to take a chance with her health. "A headache. Nausea. Dizziness. Sounds like more than stress to me."

"I'm fine now. I just got up too fast."

He dug his phone from his pocket but kept an eye on Morgan. "I'm calling Darcie to have her check you out."

"I hate to make her come out this late at night when it's not necessary."

"Isn't it?" He eyed her. "You've had plenty of chances to have this looked at. If you're not going to do it, I am."

ELEVEN

Morgan turned off the morning news and grabbed her suit jacket. She'd chosen to wear pants today, as overnight temperatures had fallen below freezing, the only sign in her life right now that Christmas Day was just around the corner. She usually embraced the holiday season with enthusiasm and joy, but it was hard to enjoy much of anything with a man stalking her.

She shrugged into the jacket, thankful the dizziness and outright nausea had passed. She wasn't back to one hundred percent yet, but she felt only a nagging headache and was mildly queasy. A good thing, otherwise Darcie would insist Morgan see a doctor today. Not that Darcie had found anything in her exam other than a bit of high blood pressure easily explained by the stress.

Still, instead of Darcie supporting Morgan's self-diagnosis, as she'd hoped last night, Darcie had taken Brady's side and was suspicious of the ongoing symptoms. Morgan wasn't alarmed, though. She knew her body best. Once the stress was gone, the symptoms would disappear.

Fresh from a shower and cleanly shaven, Brady stepped into the room. He was wearing jeans and a purple Minnesota Vikings jersey that Darcie had delivered last night along with other necessities Brady requested. Morgan didn't miss the fact that Brady's list included a second gun, a backup that he'd said he only carried on duty. Though he'd asked Jake for time off to remain at her side until the stalker issue was resolved, Brady said he'd treat this like he was on the clock and a second gun was necessary. Not a comforting thought.

"Ready to go?" His cute sideways grin nearly disarmed her.

What would it be like to be married to him? The question came out of left field, but she couldn't stop herself from considering it. To see this smile as they left together to start their day. Her heart flip-flopped and she quickly grabbed her briefcase and workout bag to get going and forget all this nonsense.

Brady stepped in front of her. "Let me clear the hallway first."

More than willing to let him check things out, she moved back. He opened the door and said something under his breath before he jerked back and slammed it, his hand immediately going for his gun.

"What?" she asked, her heart already racing.

"The stalker left another message for you," he said, sounding as if he was spitting each word out.

"Let me see it." She tried to brush past him.

He stood resolutely in her path. "I'm not letting you go out there until after I make sure the creep isn't still in the building."

She wanted to see the message, but she didn't want to risk her life. She stepped back.

"Lock the door behind me and don't open it for anyone but me." He searched her eyes for a long time, then gently cupped the side of her face. "I know you want to prove you can do everything on your own, but your life could be on the line here. So promise me you'll do as I say."

"I promise," she whispered, her skin tingling from his touch.

"After you lock the door, call Rossi and have him dispatch a patrol car." A final tight smile and he stepped out the door, closing it so quickly Morgan could only catch sight of what she thought was a black rose.

"I didn't hear the lock, Morgan," he said from the other side of the door.

She twisted it.

"Now step away from the door and call Rossi," he added.

She backed away and dialed Rossi. As she waited for him to answer, she took a seat on the sofa and stared at the envelope of photos on her table. Her mind raced over the possibilities of what awaited her in the hallway.

She knew very little about stalkers, but she had to assume a black rose wasn't a good sign. In movies and books, red usually meant infatuation, but black…

A chill settled over her.

"Stop," she warned herself. "Don't go there until you confirm the rose."

Detective Rossi answered his phone and her words tumbled out of her mouth.

Rossi muttered something she couldn't make out. "I'll get a uniform dispatched, and I'll be right behind him. Did Owens tell you to stay put behind locked doors?"

"Yes."

"Then do so. If this guy showed up with a deputy on scene all night, he's dangerous. Very dangerous."

Rossi's comment sent Morgan's stomach churning. Not for herself. She felt safe with the door locked and police officers on the way. It was Brady she was worried about. He was out there alone. Sure, he had a gun—correction, two guns—and sure, he was trained in this sort of thing, but that didn't stop her from worrying.

She shot to her feet and paced. Every noise made her jump. The building's groans. Pipes clattering. Anything and everything caught her attention. The furnace kicked on, and she nearly knocked over a table.

Sirens finally sounded nearby, and she ran to the window to see a police cruiser racing down her street. Brady stepped from the building. He'd holstered his weapon and held out his badge. He talked to the officer, then left him by his car and hurried back inside. She hadn't a clue why the officer didn't join him, but she didn't care. As long as Brady came to no harm.

She ran to the door. Considered opening it. His instructions came to mind, and she didn't think twice about doing as directed and stepping back to wait. Time ticked by slowly. She was aware of holding her breath so she let it out. She couldn't believe how thoughts of Brady in the line of fire unsettled her.

Would she be so troubled if another person was out there? She thought of the other FRS members. She'd be concerned for their welfare, but this worried? She just didn't know.

Brady pounded on the door. "It's me, Morgan. You can open the door now."

She jerked it open. He stepped over the objects on the carpet and pushed past her. He tried to close the door again, but she held fast until she could make out what was sitting on the cheerful welcome mat she'd been so excited to set in front of her very first apartment door.

She forced herself to study the items. A single

black rose lay next to a picture of her and Brady taken outside her building yesterday. The photo was torn down the middle, splitting them apart. A note card with a typed message too small to read from a distance sat next to it. Was this photo a sign that she'd put Brady in danger, too?

Her stomach heaved and she glanced up at him. "The note. Did you read it?"

He shook his head. "We don't want to touch anything until Rossi gets here."

She stood staring at him, wanting to ignore his direction. Wanting to push the other items out of the way to read the note, and at the same time, not wanting to see it at all.

He gently moved her aside and closed the door. "I get that you want to read the message. So do I, but we can't tamper with evidence. It could delay finding your stalker. The important thing right now is that you stay inside. Once backup arrives for the officer downstairs, they'll go through the building more thoroughly than I was able to do alone. Then when Rossi gets here, we'll look at the stalker's note."

Her imagination went wild, coming up with terrifying ideas of what the note might contain. They only had three days to figure out the stalker's plan before the supposed wedding on Saturday. Maybe this note would give them a lead. Filled with worry, she peered at Brady.

He rested his hands on her shoulders, the

warmth doing little to ease her fear. "Don't think about it, honey. I'm sure whatever you're conjuring up in that pretty little head of yours is far worse than what the note actually says."

Was he right, or did her stalker's message say he was coming for her and no matter Brady's protection, the stalker would succeed?

Brady held the note card, encased in a plastic evidence bag by Rossi. Brady felt like the thing was burning through the plastic, scalding his hand, and he wished he didn't have to display the card for Morgan, who stood with her hand out.

"Show me," she demanded looking strong and vulnerable at the same time.

How she did that, he couldn't figure out, but he knew her strength in the face of adversity made her a special woman. He handed her the note, her gaze instantly riveting to the page. Brady glanced over her shoulder and read the message again.

Morgan, Morgan, Morgan. You've finally left your fiancé, and now you're taking up with this guy? You're mine. He shouldn't be here. Get rid of him or I'll take care of you both. If I can't have you, no one can.

Brady couldn't pull his focus from the cardstock's vivid red color. He suspected the stalker meant it to symbolize blood.

The note fluttered from Morgan's fingers to the floor, and she wrapped her arms around her stomach. "If you don't back off, he's going to kill you. Me. Both of us."

Brady took her hand, threading his fingers with hers as he turned her to face him. "He's not getting anywhere near you on my watch."

"But what about you? He's threatening you, too. You have to stop helping me. I can't—"

"No," Brady said forcefully, making her jump and pull her hand free. "I won't leave you unprotected. Besides, the stalker would want to kill any guy who took over your protection detail from me, too. I won't put anyone else in that position."

"But you—"

"Shh." He made sure his tone was softer. "I'm a deputy. This is what I do. I can handle myself. Unless you don't trust me to protect you and want someone else on your detail." Even if she asked for someone else, he didn't know if he could step away from the woman who was coming to mean a lot to him.

"I trust you completely," she said. "I'm just worried for you."

Their eyes met, and hers reflected the same emotions churning his gut. She wanted him here as much as he wanted to be here. Something he had to make light of if he didn't want her to think that he was free to pursue the feelings growing between them.

"Why, Ms. Thorsby," he joked. "I think I might have gotten under your skin."

She scowled as if that was the worst thing that could happen to her. Maybe he'd read her reaction wrong, and she couldn't stomach the idea of him in her life in any capacity other than a bodyguard.

Rossi stepped between them and picked up the bag, putting a screeching halt to thoughts of anything but the threat.

She faced Rossi. "Will this help find the stalker, do you think?"

"We'll see. It does tell us that you need to be careful. Very careful. Don't go anywhere alone."

"No need to worry about that," Brady jumped in. "I'll be with Morgan 24/7."

Rossi turned to him. "She's lucky to have you."

"Just doing my job."

Rossi snorted. "Unless your agency's had a windfall and can provide personal protection, I doubt this has anything to do with your job."

Brady ignored the comment. "Let me know if you find prints on the note."

Morgan's eyes widened. "You can get fingerprints from paper?"

Brady nodded. "Before you get your hopes up, it's likely our guy wore gloves."

"If we find any prints, I'll compare them to Nantz's and Eckert's and let you know what we find."

"Speaking of Eckert," Brady said. "Any match to the earlier prints lifted here and in Morgan's car?"

"Unfortunately, no."

Brady's frustration grew and he wanted to snap at Rossi, but he schooled his voice. "What about the last person who sent a threatening letter? Have you had a chance to question him?"

"He's traveling on business until Friday. I'll have to wait for him to return." Rossi waved the bag. "Call me if anything else happens."

Brady couldn't stomach the thought of another incident, but as long as he remained at Morgan's side the stalker would be back, and Brady was sure this creep, the one who had terrified Morgan already, wouldn't hesitate to take his game to the next level.

TWELVE

Morgan went about her day as usual at PEA, with Brady remaining closer than before. She appreciated his presence, but his protectiveness reminded her of the black rose. The note. The torn picture. Brady in danger as he cleared the building.

She suspected it was the cause of her current nausea and the headache now heading toward unbearable. Not that she'd tell anyone. Brady would call Darcie and they'd both drag Morgan to the doctor. Her clients needed her to help them locate gainful employment. After missing work this morning to meet with Rossi, she wouldn't take off for the doctor or go home sick. Aspirin was all she needed.

She started for her cubicle without telling Brady, hoping he wouldn't see her grab the pills. Unfortunately, he stayed on her heels and leaned against the wall to watch as she sat at her desk. His body language was relaxed, as if he was bored, but his eyes were intense—warrior-like—and she knew he'd put his life on the line for her without a second thought. He was a remarkable man and she wanted to give him a hug. Maybe hold him close and warn him to take care for himself, too.

Focus. Aspirins. Now. She dug them out and turned away to swallow the pills.

He took a breath and let it out slowly before saying, "Why don't we take a break from the gym tonight?"

"Why?" she asked, making sure she didn't convey the throbbing pain pounding her head.

He pushed off the cubicle wall, his eyes now holding the strain of the day and the barest whisper of concern. "After this morning, I'd like to have you safely in your apartment before dark."

"Oh…I…" A vision of running in the dark from her assailant took the rest of her words.

Brady stood taller, his shoulders back, his hands wedged on his hips just above his holster. "It's easier to assess potential threats in daylight."

The caution in his tone made Morgan's chest ache.

He held her gaze for a long moment. "You can finish up with the clients who are waiting for you, but then I'd like to leave."

She could argue with him, but in the end, they would reach the same conclusion. As soon as Morgan helped her clients, she was going home. Without a word, she gathered her things so when she finished, they could leave right away.

Brady stood aside at the doorway but raised a cautious hand. "I don't like taking you out in the open like this, so please be aware of your surroundings. Anything seems off, let me know. And listen to my directions. Okay?"

She nodded, but a commotion down the hallway grabbed her attention. Her coworkers were shouting, and she thought she heard crying. She started in that direction.

Brady stepped in front of her. "Let me check it out first."

Had she dragged her mess into the workplace? She chewed her lip and waited, each second feeling like an hour.

She hadn't thought Brady's expression could get more serious, but when he returned, his eyes were dark with unease. "One of your coworkers—a guy named Fred—collapsed. He's not breathing."

"Fred?" she muttered as she processed the information. "He has a heart condition. I know CPR. I have to try to help."

"Someone is already doing CPR and the ambulance is on the way."

As if called up by Brady, sirens wound closer.

"Your clients are waiting, right?" Brady reminded her.

Not wanting to leave without making sure Fred was fine, she took another look down the hallway.

"Fred's in good hands and you need to think of yourself right now. Remember. It'll be dark soon."

Brady cupped her elbow and urged her to move toward the resource room.

Brady was right. She had to think of her safety. Before sitting down with her first client, she texted Lacy and asked her to provide an update on Fred as soon as possible. For the next few hours, Morgan worked with her clients, but she was distracted. When Lacy stepped through the door, Morgan quickly excused herself. Lacy's face was pale with shock and Morgan was thankful when Brady crossed the room to join them.

"What happened? Is Fred okay?" Morgan asked.

Lacy bit her lip. "He didn't make it."

Morgan's heart constricted and tears threatened. "Was it his heart?"

"I don't know. He had lunch with a bunch of us, and he was complaining about dizziness."

"Did he have a headache, too?" Brady asked.

Lacy glanced at Brady. "Yes, why?"

"Wait." Morgan switched her focus to Brady. "You're not going to try to compare my symptoms with Fred's and insist I see a doctor, are you?"

Lacy's eyes widened. "Are you having the same symptoms? Is there something going around here that we need to know about?"

"She's been dizzy and she has a headache right now," Brady answered for her. "I saw you take the aspirin."

"Of course you did," she snapped when he

didn't deserve such an attitude from her. "I've also been nauseous, and Lacy didn't mention that about Fred."

Brady ignored her and faced Lacy. "Did Fred have any other symptoms?

"He was confused and his speech was slurred before he collapsed."

"See," Morgan said. "I have neither of those symptoms."

"Fred didn't have them, either," Lacy said, meeting Morgan's gaze. "Until it was too late."

Brady stepped from his truck near Morgan's apartment and checked the surroundings. The sun was rapidly dropping toward the horizon, but he wouldn't let Morgan get out of the truck without doing a thorough threat assessment. Once confident the area was clear, he opened her door. A cold, blustery wind howled down the street, the sky was gray and dark like it might snow any minute. They'd had unusually cold and snowy winters of late. Of course, two snowfalls in one season in no way compared to his Minnesota upbringing.

They walked down the street in silence. She was still irritated at him for trying to compare her symptoms to Fred's. Brady was likely overreacting. After all, Darcie had said Morgan's symptoms could be something or nothing. They were too vague to let any doctor pinpoint her problem without a lot of time and expensive tests.

It didn't alleviate his concern for her. He was good and worried. Sure, this Fred guy had other symptoms, but Brady couldn't shake the feeling that Morgan's nausea and headache were indicators of a serious problem.

They approached her apartment building and found Darcie at Morgan's front door. Though her shift was over for the day, she wore her uniform under a heavy jacket and held a medical bag with a bright red Christmas ornament key chain. She stomped her feet to keep warm.

Morgan looked up at Brady and sighed, her breath a white vapor swirling up and over her head. Brady hadn't mentioned that he'd called Darcie before they'd left work. He couldn't. Morgan was so independent, she would have ordered him not to. Maybe he'd made the wrong decision, but he did it for Morgan's well-being.

"I had to call Darcie," he said preempting any complaint she could raise. "Please try to understand. I'm worried about you." He reached for her hand but she climbed the steps before he could touch her. She greeted Darcie, then marched straight to the elevator.

"I take it you didn't tell her I was coming." Darcie thumped Brady on the forehead. "You guys are so boneheaded, at times I wonder how you ever make it to adulthood."

He didn't bother defending himself. They all boarded the elevator in silence. Once they entered the apartment, Morgan went straight to her kitchen and Brady heard the water running.

Darcie closed the front door. "Any idea why she's reacting so strongly to this? Like maybe someone close to her died recently and now she's afraid of doctors?"

"I hadn't thought about that, but honestly, I think she sees it as a sign of weakness if she doesn't do everything on her own. So she doesn't like anyone making decisions for her."

"Who does?" Darcie asked.

"Lots of people don't mind," he said with a grin. "You, my friend, are not one of them."

"No need to tell me that." She laughed as Morgan slammed a cupboard door. "Morgan could've been in a bad relationship where the guy was overly controlling. Maybe abusive."

The thought of anyone striking Morgan put a ragged hole in his heart. "I met her former fiancé. He's a real tool, and it's not far-fetched to think he's controlling, but I didn't get an abusive vibe from him."

"Let me talk to her. See what I can find out." Darcie winked. "Assuming she doesn't toss me out of the kitchen."

"I'll come with you."

"Not unless you're a glutton for punishment."

"Fine, I'll be out here."

When Darcie disappeared into the kitchen, Brady sat on the small sofa and dug out the ornament he'd been whittling. He was getting used to Morgan's delicate furnishings, but he didn't feel comfortable making a mess so he shoved the ornament back in his pocket.

"Brady," Darcie called out, her voice unusually tight. "You're gonna want to get in here."

He charged down the hallway. Found Morgan sitting on the kitchen floor. Her arm was clutched around her waist, her face pale and sweaty. She doubled over in pain and grabbed Darcie's hand.

Darcie looked up. "I think she has kidney stones."

"Thank You, God, that it isn't more serious," Brady shouted.

"Um, Brady," Darcie said. "Kidney stones hurt almost as bad as childbirth.

"I mean Fred wasn't breathing, this is better. People don't usually die from kidney stones, right?"

"Barring an infection, no. I've called for a rig. You need to let the medics in."

"You meet them." Brady pushed past Darcie and dropped to the floor. When Morgan's pain receded, he picked her up and settled her on his lap. She curled into him like a newborn kitten cuddling its mother.

"Shh," he whispered. "I'm here, honey. It'll be okay. I promise." He rested his chin on her soft hair and looked up at Darcie. "What are you waiting for? Go meet the medics."

She arched a brow, opened her mouth as if she planned to say something, then turned and left. Brady knew she wanted to comment about his behavior with Morgan. About the way he was holding her. About the need to remain professional if he was going to do his best to protect her. But he didn't care what Darcie thought. Holding and comforting Morgan as she writhed in pain was more important than anything right now, other than keeping her stalker at bay.

"Poisoned? They think I was poisoned?" Morgan cried out as pain tore at her belly. She couldn't believe these words were coming from her mouth.

"The medical examiner suspects Fred was poisoned and your symptoms mean you may have been, too." Brady's words tumbled over each other to get out.

A fresh wave of pain radiated through her stomach. The pain meds had yet to kick in fully, and she'd been doubled over since she'd collapsed in her kitchen. Brady had been by her side in the ambulance and ER, but he'd stepped into the hallway to take a call from the ME and had just returned.

She didn't know what to say. How to put words to her thoughts. Maybe it wasn't true. "The ER tests proved I have kidney stones. Nothing else."

"Antifreeze poisoning is so rare your doctor wouldn't have even begun to consider looking for it, but the ME says that the oxalic acid in antifreeze could form kidney stones. That, combined with your other symptoms, points toward antifreeze poisoning." Brady's eyes were wild, his hands unsteady as he reached for hers. He was her tower of strength and this vulnerable, uncontrolled side of him was scaring her. "Fortunately, they can do a blood test to confirm the diagnosis and get treatment started."

She still couldn't believe it. Refused to believe it, because that meant someone had tried to kill her. "If that's true, why did Fred die and I didn't?"

"The stones don't form overnight. You'd have to ingest the antifreeze over a long period of time and at doses far lower than the level that killed Fred. As your body adjusted, it would take a larger dose to produce the nausea, headaches, dizziness and vomiting that you're now experiencing."

She shook her head, but stopped when dizziness assailed her. "So if it takes that long to form stones, I could have been poisoned for months and not known it. This is...wow...just wow."

"I've already talked to your doctor. He's on his way to get your consent for the test. Then he'll rush the lab."

Her thoughts tumbled over each other, nothing making sense right now. "How could this happen?"

"The ME said the antifreeze would have to be put in your food or drinks to mask the taste." He grimaced and held her hands tighter. "That means it's someone close to you."

Close enough to get the poison into her food. The stalker? "Can't be the stalker, right? His messages claim he loves me, so why would he want to kill me?"

"That's the same question I've been asking myself." Brady's eyes narrowed, but she saw the distress in them before they did. "And it's the question we'll need to answer if we're going to keep you safe."

THIRTEEN

Brady sliced long slivers of wood into the trash can by Morgan's bed. He'd made a complete snowman ornament while they waited for the blood test to come back. Pain medicine had allowed Morgan to fall asleep nearly an hour ago. Likely the best thing for her.

A knock sounded on the door and she shot up as if terrified. Brady dropped the ornament into his lap and planted a hand on his gun. The doctor poked his head around the door. Brady relaxed and Morgan seemed to deflate with a sigh onto her bed.

The solemn-faced doctor carried a tablet computer under his arm as he approached Morgan's bed. Brady didn't need to hear the doctor say she'd been poisoned. It was there in his somber expression.

Brady had expected this news, had told himself over and over not to react and add to Morgan's pain when the confirmation came, but he couldn't stop himself from shooting to his feet to pace. She'd actually been poisoned. Not just once, but for months now. Someone had poisoned the woman he'd come to care for far more than was good for him.

"The results confirm the poisoning," Dr. Vincent stated. "Antifreeze, as we suspected. Your levels are high. Extremely high for someone not on a slab in the morgue."

She gasped, and Brady stopped to glare at the doctor for his lack of tact.

"Guess that was as bit blunt, sorry," he said sheepishly. "The good news in all of this is that you developed kidney stones. If you hadn't, we might never have discovered the poison before permanent damage was done."

"Damage? I didn't think of that." Morgan's worried gaze flew to Brady, and he stepped closer to her.

Dr. Vincent held up a hand. "Not to worry, Ms. Thorsby. We'll begin an alcohol dehydrogenase–blocking therapy right away, along with dialysis, and we hope you'll make a full recovery."

"Hope?" Brady asked, his insides churning.

"I wish I could say a full recovery was certain, but we won't know for sure until we see how she responds to the treatment." He turned his focus back to Morgan. "You'll need to remain hospitalized for a few days so the treatment can run its course, and we can monitor your organs."

She looked up at Brady, fear now rampant in her expression.

"Don't worry." He squeezed her hand. "I'll make sure the hospital allows me to stay right here with you."

"Okay, then we'll get started." Dr. Vincent tapped the touch screen on his computer. "Let me call up your file so you can authorize the procedure, and I'll write the orders."

As Morgan and Dr. Vincent discussed the treatment, Brady paced the room trying to come to grips with the fact that he'd been with Morgan for the last three days and during that time, someone was poisoning her right under his nose. Some protector he turned out to be.

He shoved his fists into his pockets. Kept walking back and forth, back and forth, his mind whirling with questions. Who could have had access to both her and Fred's food? And why poison Fred? How did he fit into the picture?

Brady stopped to look at Morgan, lying in the bed. Small. Vulnerable. Afraid.

His heart twisted with her pain and he wanted to hold her the way he had in her kitchen. Whisper into her ear that everything would be okay. But, honestly, they were dealing with a murderer now. The stakes had been raised, and Brady needed his full focus to catch the killer.

* * *

Poisoned. The word continued to echo through Morgan's mind as the doctor left her room. She wanted to believe she was going to be okay, but she couldn't think straight enough to make sense of any of this.

Brady crossed the room and sat on the edge of her bed. He was tentative and unsure as he reached for her hand. "You scared me. After Fred died I…" He looked up at the ceiling and shook his head. "Then you were in so much pain. I thought…" His voice fell off in a tortured whisper.

The raw, unfettered anguish on his face, in his tone, brought tears to the surface that had threatened since she'd collapsed, and she could no longer control them.

"Don't cry, honey," he said, and patted her hands.

His kindness made it worse, and she started sobbing in earnest.

He muttered something under his breath and drew her into his arms. She forgot all about her medical problems and relaxed against him, clinging tightly. He stroked her back and whispered comforting words, helping her to gain control of her feelings.

She pushed back. Her tears had dampened the fabric of his shirt and she touched the spots. "I got you all wet."

He smiled, but it was weak and forced. "No problem. I won't melt."

And he wouldn't. He was strong. Tough. A protector.

She looked into his eyes. He was here for her. Holding her now and in her kitchen when she didn't know if she would live through the pain. Watching over her. Protecting her. He was quite a man, and she'd somehow let him get through the thick armor she donned after her father had insisted she couldn't make it on her own. Brady was a threat to her independence. A big one. He could break through all her defenses if she wasn't careful. That she couldn't afford. Not now. Not when she was establishing herself and had found a fulfilling life. A good life. And she wouldn't do anything to lead him on. Maybe they shouldn't even be spending any time together. She had to give him a chance to gracefully back away.

"I appreciate everything you'd done for me—being here for me—but maybe it's best if we contact Rossi to take over now." She smiled and gently removed her hand to eliminate the warm physical connection. "I'm sure you have better things to do anyway."

A curtain fell over his eyes and he leaned back. She'd hurt him, and wanted to take his hand to erase the damage, but that wouldn't help either of them in the long run. He ground his teeth together and watched her for long uncomfortable moments. She resisted squirming under the intensity.

He crossed his arms, a scowl on his face. "I'm not going anywhere until this is resolved."

"I appreciate that, Brady, really I do, but I've imposed on you enough."

"You're not imposing," he ground out. "This is what I do. My job. I'm committed to keeping you safe. Just because you're in the hospital doesn't mean your stalker can't get to you."

His comment sent a bolt of shock through her. "I didn't think about that."

"No need to. I've got it covered." His expression turned even stonier.

"But I…"

"No buts, Morgan. I'm with you until we find the stalker. End of discussion." He blew out a breath. "Now, do you want me to call anyone? Like your parents?"

Her parents? No. She shook her head.

"I'm sure they'd want to know."

She frowned. "Yes, but my dad would be here in a flash. Questioning the doctors. Bossing them around. Pushing until people did as he commanded."

"I'm sure he'd have your best interests at heart."

"I'm not sure he even knows what my best interests are. It's all about what he wants. The trial proved that." Memories of her father's demanding behavior came flooding back, to suddenly be replaced by the peace and comfort she'd found in God. Peace and comfort she'd let disappear from her life this week.

Forgive me, Father. Let me lean on You more and not on myself and Brady.

She looked at Brady. "I've really been a bad example, haven't I?"

"In what way?"

"Every time something bad has happened, I've lost it and haven't relied on God." She shook her head again. "The thing is, the trial taught me where true peace is found and I know better."

Brady didn't speak but continued to look at her, his expression sour as if he'd discovered something unpleasant. Maybe he thought she was one of those Christians who professed faith but didn't live it. Well, if he was thinking that, he was right.

She twisted her hands. "I guess unless you've gone through something like this you wouldn't understand."

"Oh, I understand all right. God got me through my tours in Afghanistan, but…" Brady paused and shrugged. "I have to admit, my life has been pretty calm since I joined the team, and I've kind of let my faith slide."

Had she done the same thing? After her life had settled into a routine, she hadn't asked God for direction as much and was often too busy to consult Him. Just like Brady.

"Who knows," she muttered to herself. "Maybe God allowed this stalker in my life to get my attention."

"You think He does that?"

She shrugged. "During the trial, one of the pastors at our church told me to thank God that I was in that crisis as God was trying to get my attention. He said that no matter how hard and how far I tried to run, God wasn't going to let me get away until I caught on to what He was trying to tell me."

"Interesting." Brady furrowed his brow and sat back, his expression saying he was a million miles away.

They fell silent for a long time when suddenly a look of resolve passed over his face. "We need to get back on point and figure out how you and Fred both ingested the poison."

Her stomach plummeted at his change in subject.

"Did you ever share any food?"

She thought back. *No. Oh, no.* It was her fault. "Fred always teased me about my energy drinks. Sort of the way you reacted to them. So I told him he could help himself to one anytime he wanted. When I went to clean up today, I found an empty bottle on the counter. I just figured I'd forgotten to take one home."

"We can test the bottles for the antifreeze."

She shook her head. "I washed them as soon as I got home so I could make more."

"Do you have other drinks from the same batch?"

"No." She let the implications of their discussion settle in. "Since this happened at work, does this mean it's Nantz, after all?"

"Could be, I suppose." Brady lifted his face in thought. "When did you make this batch?"

She thought back. "Saturday afternoon. I dropped off the bottles for the week at the office on Sunday when I went to the office to get ready for the job fair."

"Was Nantz there?"

"Yes," she answered. "In fact, he locked up after we all left."

"Okay, good. He's top on the list. What about Saturday, after you made the drinks? Were you home the entire time until you took them to the office?"

"No. My parents had an anniversary party that night."

"So someone could have broken into your apartment and added antifreeze to the bottles then. Means it could also be Eckert." Brady shook his head and added, "Or not. We just don't have enough evidence yet to point the finger at anyone."

And that's what scared her most. She had a stalker, one who they now knew wanted to kill her, and they had no more proof of his identity than the day she found the first rose and picture.

Brady stepped into the hallway to wait for Darcie, Archer and Jake to arrive. Brady had phoned them to discuss the poisoning, but instead of a lengthy phone conversation, they agreed to meet in the hallway outside Morgan's room. Brady would like to have added Cash to the mix, too, but he was on duty.

Brady leaned against the wall and caught a whiff of Morgan's perfume lingering on his shirt. He could still feel the warmth of her body pressing against him. The urge to kiss her that had lingered until she'd told him to go away.

Ha! Like that was going to happen. She may not want him around, but he was going to keep this monster away from her. This man who'd systematically poisoned her for months.

Brady pushed off the wall and paced down to the nurses' station that was decorated with a small tree and blinking lights. He flicked a quick look at the tree and instead of thinking about the upcoming holiday and embracing it for what it truly was about, all he could think of was whether Morgan would be alive at Christmas. How was that for putting his trust in God, as Morgan was saying?

Failure, buddy. Big failure.

Angry with himself for letting his emotions

take over his faith, he stormed back down the hall. When he turned, his teammates rounded the corner. Snow peppered the shoulders of their black FRS jackets. Jake was empty-handed, but Archer held a tray with coffee and Darcie carried her knitting bag in one hand while the other held a stuffed bear with a Band-Aid on its paw. She'd offered to keep Morgan company so Brady could talk to the team.

Darcie stopped in front of Brady, her gaze immediately appraising him. "How's Morgan doing?"

"Still nauseous, but the doctor said that should disappear soon."

"And you? How are you holding up?"

"Fine, why?

"This isn't just another case for you," she said eyeing him as if challenging him to deny it. "You care about Morgan. That makes it more stressful."

"That it is."

Archer handed a cup of coffee to Brady. "I figured it was going to be a long night and we can use help staying awake."

"I'll go sit with Morgan," Darcie said. "Maybe you guys should head down to the lounge."

"No," Brady said adamantly.

Jake eyed him. "If the stalker tries anything, which is unlikely at the hospital, Darcie's carrying and we've all made sure she knows how to use her gun."

Darcie patted her purse. "A break will do you good."

"Not like I'm much for sitting around."

"Fine," Darcie said. "Then take out your whittling and keep busy that way. Just take a break from always being on guard."

"I doubt I can do that until after we catch the stalker."

"Then you're at risk for burning out." She squeezed his arm. "Let us help, Brady. We want to."

"Fine," he finally said. "I'll go to the lounge and try it for a few minutes, but call me if anything happens."

Darcie rolled her eyes and pushed through Morgan's door.

Jake led the way to the nearest lounge and Brady lingered in the doorway where he could keep an eye on Morgan's door. Archer handed a cup to Jake and took the last one for himself.

"So where are we?" Jake dropped into a chair.

Brady shrugged. "I'm just not sure where to go from here. As I see it, even if we had enough evidence to get a warrant to search for antifreeze at Eckert or Nantz's place—"

"Which we don't," Jake interrupted.

"Right, which we don't, most car owners have antifreeze in their garage."

Jake nodded. "And most antifreeze is made from the same active ingredients so we couldn't link a specific brand to anything we might find at Morgan's place."

"Anyone search her house yet?" Archer asked.

"I called Rossi. His team is on it."

Jake took a long drink of his coffee, then stared over the cup. "Eckert owns a garage. That would make him more familiar with antifreeze than Nantz."

"Still, Nantz would have ready access to antifreeze."

Archer leaned forward. "If we want to hone in on the best suspect, we should look at motive. The slow poisoning likely means we're looking for someone who wanted to see her suffer. Obviously this isn't the normal behavior of a stalker who professes his love as the messages she's received would indicate."

"Are you saying we're dealing with two people here, then?" Brady snapped, sounding as frustrated as he felt.

"It could be one guy," Archer said. "He'd just be an even sicker individual who could justify poisoning her as a way to weaken her so he could prove that she needs him, or as a way to gain a sense of control over her."

Brady shook his head. "I don't get that mentally ill vibe from Nantz or Eckert."

"Remember, sociopaths can hide their behavior quite well so maybe you're not seeing it."

"Maybe." Brady leaned against the wall and let his mind wander over other people in Morgan's life that they may have missed.

"What if we tried to set a trap for the stalker?" Jake asked.

Brady perked up. "Like what?"

"No one other than the killer knows that Morgan and Fred were poisoned. When she gets out of here, she can mix up a new batch of drinks. Then she can make a container accessible at work, tell her coworkers it's a different batch and we can watch with a hidden camera. We could place one in her home, too, and maybe one at the gym. If someone bites, we'll have our suspect."

Warming to the idea, Brady smiled. "We can make that happen."

"Since Morgan has to remain in the hospital it'll give us plenty of time to get our plan together." Archer crossed his leg. "I'm guessing you'll want to stay here with Morgan, so why don't Jake and I arrange for the equipment needed to set this up."

"Thanks, man," Brady said. "Now all we need to do is finalize a plan and get Morgan on board."

They spent the next hour hashing out details and assignments, and when they'd finished Brady went back to Morgan's room to relieve Darcie.

Morgan huddled in her bed, tubes running from her neck to the machine cleaning her blood and returning it to her body. She looked so beaten down that if Darcie hadn't been in the room, he'd already have had Morgan in his arms.

Darcie stepped up to him. "Can I talk to you in the hallway?"

Brady was certain Darcie was going to give him more bad news about Morgan and his gut ached as he stepped back outside.

"I'm worried about Morgan." Darcie's eyes narrowed with concern. "The reality of being poisoned has set in and she's barely holding it together."

He shoved a hand through his hair. "Any suggestions on how to help her?"

"Just be there for her and whatever you do, don't be your usual fidgety self, pacing around the room. That'll only make it worse." She gave him an encouraging smile and quick hug. "I've always liked Morgan, so don't hurt her, okay?"

"Hurt her? I'm protecting her."

"I don't mean physically. We both know you're attracted to her, likely more, but you've got a thing about making money before getting seriously involved with a woman. Not to mention the chip on your shoulder when it comes to wealthy people. Don't lead Morgan on and then spring that little surprise on her."

"I don't plan on doing any such thing."

"I get that you're not planning it up here." She thumped his forehead. "But I saw how you looked at her just now. You're not thinking with your brain."

Darcie departed, and he stepped back into Morgan's room. She was sitting up in bed with only a small corner light on. Shadows shrouded her face, but he could hear the sounds of crying, and her shoulders were shaking.

He crossed the room and gingerly sat on the edge of her bed. "What is it, honey?"

She sniffled and shook her head.

He took her hand, held it between both of his. "You can tell me."

"It's Fred. I keep thinking if I hadn't let him have one of my drinks, he—"

"Hey, hey," he interrupted. "You can't think that way. This is all on the person who put the poison in your drinks. We'll find him and he will pay."

"I know, but—" A deep sob tore away her words.

He ignored Darcie's warning, ignored his own resolve, and carefully drew Morgan into his arms. She clung to him with her free arm and sobbed into his chest. He was aware of everything about her. Her scent. The softness of her hair. The warmth of her body. The stilling of her crying and the soft contented breathing that followed.

She didn't move. He didn't, either. Neither of them willing to part, perhaps. At least, he wasn't willing. Did she feel the same way?

He pulled back. Searched her eyes. Saw the interest burning in the depths.

"Morgan, I…" He didn't know what to say so let his words fall off.

She reached up. Caressed his cheek. Her touch was tender and electrifying at the same time.

How could she cause these reactions in him? No one else ever had and he didn't know what do to. How to act. He did know he wanted to kiss her. But as Darcie just warned, it wouldn't be fair to Morgan.

She circled a delicate hand around the back of his neck. Drew his head down.

She wanted him to kiss her. He wouldn't, couldn't, deny either of them.

He lowered his head. His lips met hers. Emotions shot through his blood. She returned the kiss measure for measure. He was lost in the kiss, and if he admitted the truth, a bomb could go off in the room and he wouldn't hear it.

Not good.

He pulled back, keeping his eyes averted from her face and slowing his breathing. If he didn't already have enough reasons not to kiss Morgan, he had to remember she was counting on him to protect her. He couldn't afford to lose his focus and let her down. Her life depended on it.

FOURTEEN

Morgan watched Brady as he talked on his phone. He sat in a vinyl recliner by the window in her hospital room, exactly where he'd been all morning. Even when the nurses came in to do their checks. Or when Lacy stopped by to visit. Even when taking phone calls. He'd sat right there as he chatted with Archer about the plan they'd hatched to trap the person poisoning her drinks.

She appreciated Brady's care and concern, but she wished he would go home so she could be alone to think. Not about last night's amazing kiss, but about how she felt after the kiss. Wanting more. Wanting him in her life despite knowing that wasn't possible.

The door suddenly flew open and her father rushed in. He locked his focus on her and crossed the room in a few quick strides. Brady's hand went to his gun as he shot to his feet.

"Dad," she said, and waved Brady off. Her mother, dressed in a linen suit, her hair perfectly in place, trailed Morgan's father into the room as she'd trailed him everywhere for as long as Morgan could remember. Always living in his shadow. A life Morgan didn't want for herself and would do everything possible to avoid.

He planted his feet wide. "I've already got them working on moving you to a private room, and I've arranged for a qualified specialist to see you."

She tightened her hands under the blanket. "How did you find out I was here?"

"Your mother stopped by your work to take you out to lunch today, but your friend Lacy said you were here with kidney stones."

"Hello, dear." Her mother gave a tight smile. "I'm sorry to hear about the kidney stones. I've heard they're quite painful."

"My specialist will get that sorted out," her father said.

"I have everything covered, Dad. I don't need or want a private room or your doctor's help. My insurance won't cover the room."

"Nonsense. I'll take care of the bill."

"No," she said firmly. "I don't want your money."

"Don't be stubborn. You may have tried to make it on your own, but this just shows how much you still need us."

The words stung, but Morgan took a deep breath and reminded herself to stay calm and firm. "You're not hearing me, Dad. I don't need your help with this. My insurance will cover most of it, and I have a perfectly wonderful doctor."

"I don't care what—"

Brady shot across the room. "Give it a rest already. She said she was fine."

"And you are?"

"This is Brady Owens. He's a—"

"A friend," Brady interrupted.

A good thing, or in the heat of arguing with her father she might slip up and say something about the poison or her stalker.

"Brady," Morgan continued. "These are my parents, Randall and Felicity Thorsby."

Her father arched a brow and stared at Brady. "You're a friend with a gun, I see."

"I'm a deputy."

"If you're carrying, does that mean you're on duty?" Her father returned his focus to her. "Is there something more we need to know about here?"

"Relax," Morgan said. "Nothing's wrong." At least not at the moment, other than her father inserting himself into her life.

"As she said, sir," Brady added, "Morgan's perfectly safe and there's no need for you to worry."

Her father didn't seem to believe Brady and focused his intense gaze on Morgan again. "You will, of course, stay with us when you are discharged."

"No." She shook her head for added emphasis. "I'm fine on my own."

Her father crossed his arms. "I won't accept that."

Brady scowled at her dad. "Morgan said no. Let it go at that." He turned his focus on her and the scowl vanished. "You can stay at the firehouse where Darcie can monitor your health."

She could think of nothing better than not having to take care of herself for a few days and spending it with the fine members of the FRS. But she couldn't accept Brady's offer. Not with her father watching. He'd see it as weak. *Her* as weak. As needing help. She wouldn't lose ground with him now. Not after she'd worked so hard to prove her independence.

Brady was about to argue the point further when the door opened again. Great. Just the person Brady didn't want to see.

Wearing another tailored suit, every hair in place, and carrying a stuffed bear plus a vase filled with white long-stemmed roses, Preston stepped in as if he belonged. He set the flowers on the table. "I hope I've given you all enough time to catch up."

"What are you doing here?" Morgan asked, sounding mad.

"I was worried about you, sweetheart." He handed the bear to Morgan who took it and set it aside without looking at it. "I hope you're coming home to recuperate with your parents."

Morgan frowned.

"Actually," Brady stepped closer to Morgan, "Morgan will be going to her apartment and if she needs any help, I'll be there for her. I've crashed on her living room floor before, I can do it again," he added to see how Preston would respond.

He clenched his jaw, but quickly blew off whatever strain he was feeling. "Doesn't sound like the smartest of plans."

"Will everyone just stop?" Morgan snapped. "I'm a big girl, and I don't need the four of you planning my life." She crossed her arms. "Now, if this is the only reason you're here, you might as well take off, as I'm not changing my mind."

Preston glared at Brady as if he was the cause of Morgan's refusal, but she'd told him no, too. Brady had to admit it hurt. Maybe she was putting on a show for her parents so they didn't find out about the stalker and poison, but it didn't feel like a show. Her anger with all of them felt real.

His best course of action was to stand back and wait until the others left, then ask her about it. He watched her interact with them and an uncomfortable vibe continued to linger in the room. Morgan shut her father down after most everything he said. He didn't look hurt by her treatment, just mad that she wouldn't go along with him.

And Preston? He was upset, but Brady wasn't sure why. Could it be that he really hadn't wanted to break up with Morgan? Just because he wasn't in town to leave the items at her house, didn't mean he hadn't been the one to poison her. He clearly fit the narcissistic personality. From what Archer said, a man of that type wouldn't look fondly on anyone who walked out on him as Morgan had done.

Brady wanted to question the guy, but Brady couldn't give Preston any indication that they knew about the poison and alert him to be on guard. Brady settled for watching the clock tick down until they departed. The door had barely closed when he stepped up to Morgan's bed. "Is there any way Preston could have access to your keys?"

"It's possible, I suppose. My mom never gave me a list of who met with my dad in his office, but Preston could be one of them."

"Can you ask your parents about the keys without making them suspicious?"

"I thought we'd ruled Preston out. Did he do or say something here to change that?"

"I'm getting a weird vibe from him."

"A vibe? That's all this is?" She shook her head. "I know him better than you and I think he's acting normal."

"Maybe you still care about him and can't see it," Brady said, and hoped she'd refute his comment.

"Trust me. There is nothing left between us other than casual friendship."

"Then you won't mind if I have Rossi run Preston's prints." Brady recovered Preston's iced tea cup from the trash. He felt Morgan's disapproving stare follow him, but he didn't care. He didn't like Preston. Not one bit. And Brady was on a mission to prove the guy's guilt, no matter what.

To Morgan's dismay, Rossi wasted no time in processing Preston's prints. A mere hour had passed before he emailed the report to Brady who handed the document to her with an I-told-you-so look on his face.

"Morgan," Brady said. "You're not saying anything."

She looked up at him. "What *can* I say? Preston's prints match the ones lifted from my house and car, but we have proof that he was out of town when those first roses were left for me."

"Do we?" Brady shoved his fingers through his hair leaving little tufts standing up. "Perhaps Rossi wasn't as thorough as he should have been. He didn't actually give me details of Preston's alibi. He just said it checked out. Maybe we need to take a deeper look."

She shook her head. "Or the prints could be from when Preston previously visited my apartment. Plus he likely touched my car when he walked me to it after dinner at my parents' house."

"I don't get you." Brady crossed his arms, frustration oozing from his pores. "You want this to end. You want us to find the person who poisoned you, and yet you won't even consider that we might need to relook at Preston."

"I can't," she fired at him.

"Why?" he shot back as quickly.

"Why? Why?" Her voice carried to the ceiling. "Because I was engaged to him, all right? What kind of judge of character does that make me if I almost married a stalker?" She crossed her arms. "It would say I can't rely on my judgment for anything. That's not something I need to hear at a point in my life when I'm striking out on my own."

Brady's frustrated look vanished. "It doesn't say that at all. You heard Archer. These men are masters at manipulating and hiding their ways." Brady sat on the edge of the bed and took her hand, the warmth of his fingers thawing hers. "If it turns out he's not who you thought he was, you can't beat yourself up about it. Just be thankful you broke it off with him when you did."

"Maybe you're right. I don't know." She sighed and took a deep breath to bolster her confidence to admit the next thing. "I still don't see Preston as a stalker, but I can see him wanting to retaliate for a perceived wrong."

"A wrong like you leaving him?" Brady's voice dropped, his hand tightened.

"Yes," she whispered as she looked down.

Brady continued to hold her hand, and with the other, he crooked a finger under her chin to lift it.

He met her gaze. Held it. "Then you consider him a possible suspect in the poisoning?"

Did she? Did she really? "I want to say no, but you're right. We need to at least keep him on the suspect list."

"I know that was hard to admit, but it's a step in the right direction." Brady smiled as he squeezed her hand. "Are you up to helping me set a trap for him?"

"A trap?" She jerked her hand away.

Brady looked like she'd slapped him, and he slid back. "We have to find out, Morgan. One way or another, we have to find out."

She resisted sighing. "What do you want me to do?"

"I'd like you to call Preston. Tell him you had to change the locks on your apartment and car. Ask if he'll stop by here to pick up a new set of keys and take them to your father since you can't leave the hospital. When Preston arrives, I'll tail him to see if he uses the keys or has copies made before he hands them over to your dad."

"That sounds so underhanded."

"And you think poisoning you isn't under-handed?"

She imagined the scenario playing out. Seeing Preston use the keys to leave a rose or picture. The thought sent a shiver over her body. "No, it is, but…"

Brady took both of her hands this time, his big,

strong fingers wrapping around hers. He watched her for long moments, his eyes seeking something. "I get it, Morgan. Trust me, I do. It's hard to treat someone you once cared about this way."

"Exactly."

"I'm asking you to take a big step. Forget about your past with Preston and help me either rule him out or catch him in the act." Brady smiled, his expression comforting. "Can you do that for me?"

With the way he was looking at her, his eyes soft, his smile warm, his expression caring, she'd agree to just about anything. Even this. She nodded.

"Good. Thank you. It's the right thing to do. I know it is." He released her hand. "I'll get an extra set of keys made. You call Preston. Okay?"

"Yes," she said, feeling like she was betraying a friend. But if Brady was right, Preston could be the man who tried to kill her, and she had to learn the truth no matter how painful it might be.

"Don't worry, I got this," Cash said outside Morgan's door, but his words gave Brady little comfort.

He didn't want to leave Morgan in anyone's hands. Not even Cash's. As a former Army Delta, he was a force to be reckoned with and anyone intent on harming Morgan would likely take one look at Cash and turn the other way.

Still, things could go wrong quickly. Brady

ought to know. He'd performed the same security duty for Cash's fiancée, Krista. Done everything in his power to care for her just as Cash would have, and she was still almost killed.

The memory of her near death cautioned Brady to be even more diligent and careful with Morgan. "I trust you, man, but you trusted me, too. Then my detail for Krista went wrong. Remember?"

Cash ran a finger around the collar of his shirt and tugged. "Won't likely ever forget it, but it all ended okay."

"Eventually." Brady stared at Morgan's door. "Maybe I should stay and let you follow Preston."

Cash lifted dark eyebrows. "I'd be glad to do it for you, but if it turns out this guy poisoned Morgan, do you really want to miss out on bringing him to justice?"

"Of course not," Brady answered without thinking. "If he's our guy, then I want to see the cuffs slapped on his wrists and the sorry excuse for a man thrown into the back of a patrol car."

"Exactly."

"Okay, fine. But I want you to stand right next to Morgan when she hands Preston the keys. And then I expect a text from you every five minutes telling me things are okay."

Cash arched an eyebrow and stared at Brady.

"What?" Brady asked.

"You've got it bad, man. Real bad."

"You mean Morgan? It's purely professional,"

he said, but his words rang false even to his own ears.

"Yeah, right." Cash took a step closer. "Wasn't too long ago that you were warning me to think with my head and not my heart. You should consider your own warning before you do something stupid that could get you or Morgan killed."

Brady appreciated Cash's concern, but Brady didn't need a warning. He knew what the stakes were here. Morgan's life was in the balance, and he'd take no chances.

He clapped Cash on the shoulder. "Thanks, man, but I got this."

"See that you do. Keep your head on a swivel." Brady smiled at the cop term meaning to continually check your surroundings. "After all," Cash continued. "I'd hate to lose my favorite jokester."

"I know, right?" Brady grinned. "'Cause you couldn't tell a joke to save your life."

Cash socked Brady in the arm, and he feigned discomfort before taking off down the hallway. His smile fell the minute he rounded the corner and went into sniper mode. He may not have a rifle in his hands, but he did have a target to take down. Preston. If the guy made any wrong move, Brady would have an officer on scene to arrest him so fast Preston wouldn't know what hit him.

Brady stepped outside and went straight to the spot he'd scouted earlier. Finding a place to watch Preston was just like locating a sniper blind, except Brady wanted to be closer so he could easily tail Preston after he picked up the keys.

Brady took cover behind a half wall surrounding a large air conditioning unit and watched. Preston soon double-parked his shiny silver Lexus at the entrance and hopped out. He whistled as he strutted inside. Brady almost gave up his stance and charged after the man, but he settled for texting Cash and warning him to take care. Ten minutes later, ten long minutes, Brady saw Preston step out. He was smiling and swinging the keys around his index finger.

Brady didn't like the change in Preston's attitude. Didn't like it one bit. Brady also didn't like thinking about what Morgan had said or done to put the smile on Preston's face. Hands fisted, Brady headed to his truck and was soon rumbling along behind Preston's spotless ride. He hung well back as they eased through the city streets full of traffic. Preston made a few turns, pointing his car in the direction of Morgan's apartment.

Brady's gut churned and he inched closer to Preston so he wouldn't lose him. Preston pulled to the curb in front of a florist shop, and Brady's mouth dropped open.

Could he be buying roses? Was it really going to be this easy to catch the guy?

Brady parked down the block where he could keep an eye on Preston, who got out of his car, looked up and down the street, then strutted into the shop. Brady tried not to get excited. Preston was buying flowers, but it remained to be seen if they were red roses.

Brady fixed his gaze on the door. Waiting. Watching.

His phone chimed a text, and he jumped in his seat.

"Get a grip, man," he warned himself and grabbed the phone.

Cash confirmed all was well at the hospital, and Brady's mind drifted back to the conversation with his buddy. Brady got that he was attracted to Morgan. Totally attracted, but had he fallen for her? For a woman who was wrong for him in every way?

If he had, he was in for a world of hurt. She would never see him as an equal to the men she'd been raised with. Even if she somehow did accept him, her father never would. No way. Brady had seen the guy in action. He was all about his image and pedigree. And how could Brady ever fit in her life, with her exclusive club membership and BMW? He couldn't—that was all there was to it.

Preston stepped out of the shop carrying a long white box. Had to be long-stemmed red roses. Or maybe black. The thought made Brady angry. This guy had at one time told Morgan he loved her and had given her a ring. Asked her to spend the rest of her life with him. Now this? Unbelievable. Morgan was going to be devastated.

Preston slid the box into the back of his car and set off. Brady hung back, hoping he was wrong and Preston had just happened to be buying flowers. Though Brady would be glad for Preston to be the stalker, it would hurt Morgan, and she didn't need additional pain.

Brady prayed for comfort for her should this be true. Maybe he should be praying for Preston to drive on by Morgan's apartment complex, instead.

Preston swung into a parking space down the block from Morgan's place and Brady reiterated the prayer for her comfort while he kept his eyes on Preston and grabbed his phone from the dash. He pressed speed dial for Rossi. Brady would love to personally charge after Preston and haul him in, but Brady had no jurisdiction here and he wouldn't risk Preston getting off on a technicality.

The moment Rossi answered, Brady explained the situation. "I need you or a unit at Morgan's apartment, stat."

"I can have uniforms over there in few minutes, and I'll be right behind them," Rossi replied.

"Make sure the officer doesn't run his lights or siren to spook Preston." This wasn't the kind of call that would suggest lights and siren, but Brady wasn't taking any chances.

Rossi snorted. "Goes without saying. See that you're as cautious. This guy's got money, and he'll fight the arrest. I want it to be a righteous collar so don't proceed without me."

Brady agreed to hang back and disconnected. Preston got out of his car, straightened his tie and suit coat, then bent into the backseat to retrieve the box. He looked around before proceeding to the apartment building, calmly walking as if on a Sunday stroll.

Brady waited, his imagination running wild, envisioning Preston going inside Morgan's building. Into her apartment. Standing over her with a camera while she was sleeping.

Preston stepped inside the door. Brady's gut clenched and a low growl sounded from his chest, surprising him at how much this was affecting him. It was all he could do to sit there and wait for Rossi or the patrol car to arrive.

"C'mon, c'mon, c'mon," he grumbled as he looked down the street for the cruiser. Preston wasn't going to get away with this. They had to catch this creep in the act and stop him once and for all.

FIFTEEN

At the Portland Police Bureau's Central Precinct, Brady stared through the viewing window at Preston. Sitting behind a metal table, his posture was perfect. His clothes perfect. His chin jutted out in a smug expression. Brady would like to be sitting across from the guy, grilling him. Making him talk. Making him admit to his plan to harm Morgan. But Rossi nixed it because Brady had no jurisdiction here. He did let Brady watch through the one-way glass. That was something, anyway.

"I wasn't doing anything wrong." Preston's chin lifted higher. "I was just making sure the apartment was clean for Morgan's homecoming and leaving flowers to freshen up the place for her."

"Why red roses?" Rossi asked.

"Why not?"

"Ms. Thorsby told us you usually gave her white roses."

His eyes flashed wide but he quickly masked

his surprise. "Guess I got her confused with my current girlfriend. She likes the red ones."

Brady felt certain Preston was lying and Brady would be sure to follow up with Natasha.

The door shot open. A regal-looking silver-haired man in a quality black suit stepped into the room and slapped a business card on the table. "My client is done answering your questions. Charge him or we're leaving."

Rossi glanced at the card then came to his feet. "If you insist, I'll be glad to charge him with trespassing."

"I didn't break in. I had keys." Preston's face was a mask of anger.

"Ah, but see, Ms. Thorsby said she didn't give you permission to enter. You were supposed to deliver those keys to her parents. I'm sure she'll be happy to issue a signed statement or testify to that fact. So, keys or not, charges will be filed."

The lawyer sneered. "Fine, bring charges, but you're the one who's going to look like a fool here."

"Better a fool than a stalker." Rossi looked down on Preston, holding the other man's attention for a long moment. "Or a killer."

"A what?" Preston's voice rose.

"Ms. Thorsby has been poisoned for months."

Preston's self-important facade disappeared for a moment. "I didn't poison her. I'm not a killer."

"Guess we'll find out, won't we." Rossi slid

a piece of paper across the table to the attorney. "Our search warrant for Mr. Hunter's home and office. You'll find everything in order." Rossi pivoted and stalked out of the room.

Brady met him in the hallway. "Please say I can come along to toss the smug jerk's place."

"You know better than to ask. Hunter's lawyer is one of the best and if we hope to keep Hunter locked up, we have to do this by the book."

Brady wanted to march into the interrogation room and shake the truth from Preston, but that would only give the guy a reason to press charges against Brady and claim police brutality, getting his case tossed out. The very last thing Brady wanted when they had no other leads on finding the creep who was putting Morgan's life in danger.

Morgan cringed under her father's wrath. He'd been angry with her before, but never like this. His eyes were bulging, spittle clung to the corners of his mouth and his face was crimson as he ranted over her role in Preston's arrest.

Cash must have been worried for her safety because he stepped closer, his body ready to swing into action in her defense.

Despite her father's hurled anger, Cash kept her feeling protected. She'd been so lucky when she'd met the FRS team. They were all strong, honest and true, with compassion for one another and those they helped. Everything she'd wished for in her family but had never found. Things and possessions always came before people. Even her father's defense of Preston was more about getting Preston to take over the company than it was about caring for Preston as a person.

Her heart shattered at the realization, and she needed to get her father out of the room before she broke down in tears. "I'm sorry if this caused you grief, Dad, but Preston broke the law."

"Because you set him up." Her father continued to glare down on her. "Don't you ever think before doing things?"

She forced herself not to cringe and to stay strong. "If he's cleared of all charges except trespassing, I'll drop those charges, and he'll be okay."

"Really? Really?" Her father crossed his arms. "You think arresting a man with Preston's status and means won't be a problem for him? Tongues will be wagging at the club. At the gym. It's going to be a PR nightmare for both of our companies. All because you got a crazy thought about him being a stalker and poisoning you." He shook his head.

"It's not a crazy accusation, Dad. I *have* been stalked. I was poisoned, and Preston did use my keys to enter my apartment without permission. He was caught red-handed, as they say."

"But he's family and you had him arrested before even talking to him. Before calling me to resolve this in a civilized manner. Unbelievable."

"It's quite believable, sir." Brady had come in the door, and Morgan hadn't even heard or seen him. Her father spun on Brady, but he stood strong, his shoulders back, his feet planted wide on the floor, his expression tough and unyielding. "Preston is a prime suspect or he wouldn't have been charged, and I'm confident the search of his home and work will provide the proof we need."

"Search?" Her father's voice rose but choked off at the end. "You can't be serious. You got a judge to sign off on such a crazy thing?"

Brady took a deep breath. Met Cash's gaze where he stood on the other side of the room. Motioned for him to take a hike.

"He's a piece of work," she heard Cash whisper as he passed her father.

Brady scowled and waited for Cash to exit, then faced her father again. "A judge found merit in our request so it's time for you to reconsider your take and step it down a notch. And—" Brady drew out the word "—did you ever think it might be more important for you to ask if Morgan was going to be all right or if the poison caused any lasting damage rather than wondering if Preston is going to have a soiled reputation?"

He turned back to Morgan. "Has it?"

Morgan hated that his tone hadn't softened in the least. "Not that doctors can tell at this point."

"Good, but that doesn't excuse your actions. You've taken this independence thing too far,

Morgan. It's time to come back to Thorsby Mill where you belong. Drop the charges against Preston and offer to take your rightful place as his fiancée. I'm sure when you do, Preston will break off his engagement to Natasha for you."

"This isn't a whim, Dad." Morgan crossed her arms. "I'm never coming back to my old job. Even if I wanted to, I can't. My faith won't allow it."

"What?" His voice shot up. "Faith? What in the world are you talking about?"

"God has a purpose for me and it's not to defend the company. It's to help struggling people get a leg up in life." She smiled. "I've not only helped people, but I've found more fulfillment and happiness these last few months than in all my years representing the mill."

"Fine. Forget the job. Just move back home where Preston and I can keep an eye on you. If you'd never left, something like this wouldn't have happened."

Her mouth dropped open and she sputtered as she tried to wrap her mind around her father's accusation. "You're blaming me for having a stalker?"

"Not blaming you, just saying a stalker would never get near you in our compound."

"Living in your compound isn't living. It's enduring. Enduring your desire to make me into the perfect socialite you always wanted me to be." She eyed him. "It's time you realize no matter what you try to do, I can't and won't be that woman. I am living on my own and loving it." She tried to put enthusiasm into her tone, but in all honesty, the "alone" part hadn't been as grand as she had hoped. But once this stalker thing was over, she'd be fine.

"We'll see about that." He fisted his hands. "So far I've let you keep the car. The gym and club memberships. If you really want to be on your own, then give them up."

She grabbed her purse from the table and dug out her key ring. She pulled the BMW key free and slapped it on her father's palm. "I can always take MAX and save up for a car of my own. And I can work out elsewhere. Now, if you don't mind, I need to rest."

He stared at her and her stomach churned. "Think about what I said about dropping charges against Preston. It would be in your best interest to comply." He pivoted and marched toward the door, shouldering Brady out of the way as he passed.

Brady looked down at her, his eyes filled with pity—the last thing she needed.

"You don't need to feel sorry for me," she said, making sure she sounded strong when her insides were quivering like gelatin. "I've known my father was this mean-spirited for a long time. I just wasn't willing to admit it until lately. But it doesn't matter. Not at all. I'm on my own. Starting my life over as I want. I don't need his money or things.

He may live for what money can buy—think he's a better man because of his wealth—but that's not important to me at all. Never has been. In God's eyes, we're all equal and that's all that matters to me."

Brady's eyes cleared and he smiled, but she had no idea what he found to be happy about in her ongoing struggle with her father. Maybe he was humoring her little tirade.

"Listen to me going off like this," she said. "I'm sorry. I guess I'm still letting Dad get to me. That will change. Once we resolve this stalking issue, I'll go back to my life. To my job and apartment. Without his interference. I'll be on my own again, and nothing is going to stand in my way. Nothing."

Brady seemed to deflate at her comment. She didn't get what was going on in his brain, but he turned away before she could ask.

He sat in the chair in the corner and took out his phone. "I'd like to invite the team over to talk about Preston. If you're not up for seeing them, we can talk in the hallway, but I'd like to get their input on this development and I'm not leaving you alone."

"Actually, I'd be glad to have the company."

"Then I'll get Jake on the phone and arrange it."

As he talked with Jake, she watched Brady from under her lashes. He'd been there for her every step of the way and didn't ask for anything in return. This was so foreign to the world she'd been raised in. The whole team was like that.

"They're on their way." Brady shoved his phone into his pocket and dug out the snowman he'd been carving. "Darcie's going to smuggle in a container of her famous chicken tetrazzini for you."

"That will be nice." The strain of her father's tirade suddenly hit, and she felt weary to the bone. "I think I'll rest until they get here."

Concern washed over his face. "Can I get you anything?"

"No. Just… Brady." She peered at him. "Thank you."

"For what?"

"For being you. For being here for me. For everything. Thank you." Their gazes met and held. She felt the electricity in the air and for the first time, she wished things could be different. That she could give in to her heart and curl her finger to beckon him across the room. To kiss him and tell him that he meant more to her than she'd thought possible.

But after today…after her father…after his hurtful words, her quest to get her life onto a firm foundation before pursuing a relationship was even more important, and she couldn't let feelings for Brady get in the way.

SIXTEEN

Brady watched a nurse prepare Morgan for discharge as he stretched his neck and tried to work out the kinks from a night in the hospital recliner. The nurses had offered to bring him a cot, but he wouldn't have slept much anyway. When he wasn't watching the door for trouble, he'd been pondering Morgan's statement from last night. She'd said she'd go back to her life alone and nothing was going to stand in her way. Nothing.

Her statement shouldn't have had any impact on him, but it had bothered him big-time. Even this morning, as he whittled away on the next snowman, he let her comment run through his head. She wanted to be alone. She didn't want a man in her life. Any man. This was said almost in the same breath as her statement about not caring about money or things. Saying people were all equal in God's eyes.

Bombshell. She didn't care about Brady's past. About the things he'd let mark him all his life. Not physically, but he'd listened to the mean things other kids and people said about him and his mother, and he'd let them define him.

What had he been thinking all these years? Buying into their garbage was like taking poison and expecting the people who hurt him to get sick. But they didn't. They went on with life as if nothing happened. They probably didn't remember the hurt they'd inflicted while he'd let it hold him back. People judging him for his profession could well be the reason he was freezing at the trigger, too. Well, not anymore. God willing.

Can You help me? Help me forget the past. Move forward.

Hopeful for a change in his take on life, he glanced at Morgan. Wished she could get over the same hurt with her father.

And help Morgan do the same thing.

The urge to wrap her in his arms and whisk her out of there, to take her home to the team where she'd feel cared for and valued for who she was, was almost too much for him. He started on the snowman. Slicing hard. Quickly. Furiously. Small strips of wood flew everywhere. Making a mess and he didn't care. All he cared about was releasing his frustrations.

The older nurse turned to look at him. "What are you making?"

He held out the chunk of wood that didn't look like much right now. "Christmas ornaments. I give a boxed set to my friends every year." He dug a finished snowman from his pocket. "Here's one that's done."

She took it and studied it. "It's amazing. My grandpa whittled. You don't see many people doing it these days." As she handed it back, she gave him a pointed look as if asking for more information.

"No, you don't," Brady responded, but didn't continue though she kept looking at him. He never told people that he'd taken up this particular hobby as a kid because it was free and they couldn't afford all the sporting equipment and things the other kids had to pass the time.

"So, you're almost ready to release Morgan?" He changed the subject.

"Once I get her discharge instructions, she'll be good to go." She turned her focus back to removing the tape holding Morgan's IV needle.

Brady caught Morgan's attention. "I don't suppose you'd reconsider staying at the firehouse. Skyler and Logan are on their honeymoon and you can stay in their condo. You wouldn't be putting anyone out and you wouldn't have to hang out with all of us if you didn't want to. Though I think it might be good for you to be around people who care about you."

At the look of surprise on her face, he regretted mentioning the last bit. He hadn't meant to, but she deserved to know there were people in her life who wanted to help her with no strings attached. He could almost see the thoughts running through her head.

"I think staying at the firehouse sounds like a good idea," she finally said.

Her simple words flooded his heart with happiness. The rush of emotion surprised him, and he needed some breathing room.

He jumped to his feet and headed for the door. "I'll be out in the hallway if you need me."

"Don't tell me needles make you squeamish?" Morgan teased.

"Nah, they don't bother me," he said, and pulled open the heavy door without making eye contact.

The way I'm thinking about you is another story. He let the thought chase him out of the room and hoped it would stop distracting him by the time she was ready to step outside where if they were wrong about Preston, her stalker could be waiting for her.

Morgan had barely been discharged when she walked into PEA's building, carrying fresh energy drinks made at her apartment. With each step, she wondered if she had the strength or might drop to the ground. The nurse had warned her to take it easy, but Morgan had to deliver the drinks to set up the sting. They could wait a day for her strength to improve, but the search of Preston's home and office turned up nothing, and Rossi was starting to think they were wrong about Preston. That her stalker was still out there. She didn't want to waste a minute trying to put an end to being stalked.

She went straight to the refrigerator and set the neatly labeled drinks on the top shelf, then headed to her cubicle. As much as she knew spending time with Brady wasn't a good idea, she still wished he was with her, giving her the sense of security she always felt when he was around. But he believed it would put her coworkers on edge if he came inside so, instead, he remained in his truck.

Lacy poked her head around the cubicle doorway. "You're back. I didn't think you were supposed to come in yet."

"I'm not, but I wanted to turn over a few clients to you so they don't fall through the cracks." Morgan felt as if she was lying to her friend, but technically she wasn't, as she *did* want to check in on her clients.

"You shouldn't have bothered." Lacy watched Morgan carefully. "I've got everything under control."

"I'm sure you do, but you know me. Just wanted to double-check." Morgan nodded at the chair by her desk. "Have a seat, and we'll run through the client list."

Lacy sat. "Who do you want to talk about first?"

Morgan opened the first client file and they

worked down the list until lunchtime. Morgan wasn't hungry, but as Lacy sat back and stretched, her stomach grumbled. The girl had an appetite that would even challenge the men of the FRS.

"I'm planning to order a pizza," Lacy said. "Will you still be here and want to share it with me?"

"Thanks, but I'm set with this." Morgan held up her drink. She'd added blueberries this time, making the liquid a bright purple. She wanted the color to tip off her coworkers that she'd made a change.

Nantz walked past the cubicle, then did a double take and backed up. "Blueberry, huh?"

She forced out a laugh. "And here I thought you'd be surprised to see me."

"That, too, but man, what's in that thing?" He smiled. "It's glowing an alien color."

She chuckled again, but her mind was all over the fact that he took particular notice of her drink, which is what she'd hoped to accomplish.

"I don't know how she comes up with the combinations." Lacy mocked a shudder.

Another coworker stopped to welcome her back and soon a small group huddled around her cubicle. She assured them she was fine and when they departed, she settled down to finish the list with Lacy.

Morgan glanced at the clock. Noon. She'd been there long enough, and though she wouldn't admit it to anyone, she was wiped out and needed to rest.

She grabbed her belongings. "Thanks for humoring me on the list, Lacy. I'll rest easier. You can reach me on my cell if you need anything."

"I won't bother you," Lacy said firmly as they walked to the door together.

"Just don't be afraid to call if you need to." Morgan stepped into the sunshine, pausing to let it warm her for a moment, then crossed the alley to Brady's truck.

He wore an earpiece and a mic hung on a cord around his neck. He was talking to Jake and Archer, who sat in a carpet-cleaning van down the alley. In addition to placing cameras here, they'd put them in the gym and her apartment, too, and they were monitoring all the camera feeds.

"I'm signing off now to take Morgan home. Call me if anything happens." He pulled out the earpiece and tossed it into the cupholder.

She buckled her seatbelt and swiveled toward him. "Anyone take the bait?"

"Not yet." He frowned. "Maybe now that you're gone, something will happen here." He shifted into gear. "Did it seem like any of your coworkers were onto the real reason for your hospital stay?"

"No, and I even talked to Nantz. He was his usual self." She frowned. "I hate that we're keeping the poisoning from everyone. And I especially hate that we haven't told them Fred's real cause of death."

"I get that, but we can't risk them knowing."

"I know," she said, and let the conversation drop.

"On the plus side, Rossi just called. Eckert was hauled in last night for a bar fight. He had a set of lock picks in his pocket."

She shot forward in excitement. "Meaning he knows how to pick a lock and could have gotten into my apartment?"

Brady held out a hand. "Hold up. Don't get too excited yet. Eckert has the tools and the skills, but we still don't have anything to connect him to your apartment. And he's claiming he has them because he's into locksport."

"What's that?"

"It's a sport where guys try to defeat locking systems."

"You're kidding, right?"

"I'm serious. They have groups to share knowledge plus participate in activities and contests. He said his former brother-in-law is a locksmith and got him started. Rossi said it checks out."

She sat back. "Still, we have a guy who clearly knows all about antifreeze and could break into my car and apartment. Since Preston seems iffy now, Eckert sounds like our best lead."

"Rossi thinks so, too. It's illegal to own lock-picking tools with the intent to use them in a burglary. Eckert claims that's not what he was doing, but it allows Rossi to hold him for additional questioning while Rossi investigates. It may not pan out, but at least we have a lead and Rossi has reason to dig into Eckert's background more."

She nodded.

"Rossi also said that he finally interviewed the last guy who sent a threatening letter. He was traveling during the times in question. So that rules out all of the people from the lawsuit who sent threats."

"I'm glad it's not one of them," she said. "I'd hate for more lives to be ruined."

All the talk of who was trying to kill her took the last bit of her energy. She leaned back and closed her eyes. The doctors said she would feel weak and tired, not only from the poison but from the dialysis, but her lack of energy surprised her, as did falling asleep for the drive to her apartment where she packed a suitcase.

At the firehouse, Brady held her elbow as he escorted her up the steps to Skyler's condo. He carried her suitcase in the other hand. Morgan knew she should shrug off his help to assert her independence, but honestly, she needed him right now and liked his help. Problem was, she also liked the warm feel of his hand on her arm.

Brady unlocked the condo door and stepped back. "Skyler says you should make yourself at home."

Morgan whipped around to look up at him. "Don't tell me you called her on her honeymoon."

"Are you kidding? I'd like my head to remain

attached to my neck." He chuckled. "They're coming back tomorrow night, and she called Darcie to ask her to do a favor. Girl stuff, she said." He rolled his eyes.

"Hey, now." She grinned. "Girl stuff is important."

"If you say so." He laughed again, and his smile warmed her to the core.

She quickly averted her eyes and caught sight of a Christmas wonderland. "Wow." She turned in a circle to take in the stockings on the fireplace, two tall trees and garland mixed with small candles strung everywhere else. "It's like a magazine."

"Skyler loves Christmas. Her parents never celebrated the holiday so she goes overboard with it."

"I can understand that."

"Your parents weren't big on Christmas, either?"

Morgan shook her head. "Just the opposite. We had party after party, but they were for grown-ups and business associates. No children. The house had to be professionally decorated, and I wasn't allowed to touch anything." She circled the room and ran her fingers over soft pine boughs. "But this? This all looks very touchable and fun."

He didn't speak, so she turned to look at him and found him staring intently at her.

"What?" she asked, almost afraid to hear his answer.

"You sound so excited. Like a little kid. But you only have one tiny tree at your place." He paused as if thinking about going on. "It looked perfect to me. Like you described your parents' decor."

What? Perfect? Her? She flashed him a surprised look and considered how not including any memories from her past in her apartment had made it barren and sparse, like a model house rather than a real home. "I guess maybe I embraced more of my parents' lifestyle than I thought. But when I have children, you better believe the whole place will be filled with decorations, presents and, most importantly, love."

He suddenly sobered and swallowed hard. She had no idea what she'd said to change the atmosphere.

"I should let you rest," he said. "I'll be downstairs in the office. I want to check the video feed from our cameras and do more research on Eckert." He rested his fingers on her cheek and looked deeply into her eyes. He seemed to come to a conclusion before he took a deep breath and blew it out. "Call me if you need anything. Anything at all."

"I will," she said, but she decided she wasn't going to call him for anything that wasn't life threatening.

At the door he turned. "We're pretty secure here, but lock up after me, just in case."

She closed the door and twisted the dead bolt, then went straight to the bathroom to slip into a pair of yoga pants and T-shirt. She didn't feel right about sleeping in Skyler's bed so she dropped onto the sofa with a soft pillow and fuzzy blanket. She'd thought she might need to work on emptying her brain of the craziness that was her life. Empty it of the feel of Brady's touch. But her eyes were heavy, and she quickly drifted off to sleep.

She dreamed of a blazing fire in Skyler's fireplace, the Christmas stockings hanging over it. The warmth of the fire felt so real that she tossed off her blanket. Her feet tangled in the fabric and she struggled to push it off. Her throat felt dry and parched, and a cough started deep in her chest. She must have slept with her mouth open. She was almost too tired to get a glass of water, but it was so dry. So hot. She heard a sound. Crackling. Near the floor. She coughed again, her whole chest heaving with exertion. She forced her heavy eyelids open.

Flames licked at the end of sofa. The drapes. The carpet.

"Fire," she called out, her dry throat leaving the word nothing more than a whisper. She drew her feet under her body and shot a look around the room.

Smoke surrounded her, billowing up in clouds to obscure her vision, the heat intensifying. Searching. Destroying.

"Help," she called out, but knew the concrete walls would muffle her cries.

Panic welled up. Flowed over. Her heart started racing.

She searched for an exit. A way out. The thick smoke stung her eyes. They watered and blurred her vision. She blinked hard, but could see nothing.

What should she do?

Father, please help me. Please.

Drop to the floor, she remembered. But flames circled her as if the fire was set to consume her.

Of course it had been. The poison hadn't worked. This was the killer's second option. Had to be.

She frantically scanned for a way out. Anything. The door. The window. Both were blocked.

Her throat closed as panic settled in. The irony of her situation wasn't lost on her. Here she was in a firehouse, and barring an act of God, a fire was going to take her life.

SEVENTEEN

Something felt off to Brady. He didn't know what. Just a sixth sense that he'd developed in the marines. It had kept him alive for two tours in Afghanistan, and he'd learned to trust it. He had to heed the feeling and check on Morgan.

He left behind the research he'd been conducting on Eckert and stepped into the family room. A hint of smoke tainted the air. A fireplace.

Maybe…or… Morgan!

He charged to the top of the stairs. Saw fingers of smoke creeping under Skyler's front door.

Dear God, no. Not Morgan.

Running, Brady dug out the keys from his pocket, then his phone to call 911. He blurted out the situation and listened as the operator confirmed his call.

"Hurry," he said, dropping his phone and grabbing the knob. It was hot to the touch. He released it. Inserted the key in the lock.

"Morgan!" he shouted as he felt the edges of

the door. Not that it mattered if flames made the door hot enough to burn his hand. He was going in for Morgan. He turned the knob and used his shoulder to press the door partway open. Flames licked around the corner and up the side.

He closed the door, ripped off his shirt and tore it into shreds. He tied strips around his hands and his mouth. After a deep breath, he shouldered the door open again.

The entire room was in flames. Smoke obscured his view of the space.

Morgan. His heart refused to beat.

"Morgan," he screamed.

"Here," her weak voice came from the middle of the living room.

He heard the hallway smoke detector go off. Good. Jake would be notified of the fire. Brady didn't think twice but charged through the flames. Got low, below the smoke. He felt the heat. Inferno hot. Licking at his bare arms. He ignored it. Moved across the polished concrete floor, thankful it wasn't wood.

"Call out, Morgan," he shouted. "I can't see you."

"Here," her voice came from close by.

He dug deep for strength. Crossed the distance. Felt around. Found her on the sofa curled into a ball. He grabbed her in a hug. "Hold on, honey. I'll get you out."

He lifted her over his shoulder, then reversed

course. Hand by hand, inch by inch, he crawled. Flames crackled around him. Smoke choked off his oxygen. Morgan's, too, as she gasped for breath. The smoke got to him. Dragging him down. He felt like giving in. Collapsing.

No. Stay with it. Get Morgan to safety.

He dug even deeper. Surged forward, his body landing in the hallway. He pulled in a deep breath, but the air was still contaminated, and he coughed so hard he thought he'd heave out a lung. He managed to get to his feet and move down the hallway to cleaner air where he set Morgan down. She was coughing, but dragging in air. He took deep breaths of his own while scanning her from head to toe looking for any injury. She'd tied a scarf over her mouth and nose to hold off the smoke. Soot covered her face, but she hadn't suffered any burns.

"Your leg," she screamed.

He looked down surprised to see flames engulfing his jeans. He dropped to the floor. Tried to pat it out. Morgan leaped on top of him, extinguishing the flames with her body.

She was quite a woman. Brave beyond words. He couldn't believe she'd fallen onto fire for him.

The reality of the event hit him. He could have lost her. Fear coursed through his body, and he pulled her into his arms. Held her as they both worked to get fresh air into their lungs.

They lay there together until firefighters

pounded up the steps and insisted they exit the building. Together they stumbled down the stairs and outside. An EMT rig was pulling in, Darcie launching herself out the door before the vehicle stopped. She rushed across the parking lot. Scanned them from head to toe as he'd done with Morgan, but Darcie was looking at both of them with a clinical eye. She grabbed Brady's hand and dragged him to the back of the rig. Her partner had the door open.

"On the gurney," she demanded.

"Morgan first."

"Morgan doesn't have any burns and Mickey here will see to her breathing."

Brady let Darcie minister to him. He knew it was hopeless to argue when she was in her madmother mode. As he lay there, the rest of the team arrived one by one. Jake nodded at Brady, acknowledging his survival in Jake's usual terse way, and then he marched to the front door where he met with a firefighter.

Archer and Cash stepped up to the gurney.

"If Cash hadn't been with us," Archer said, a snarky smile on his face, "I would've wondered if he was cooking again."

Cash shook his head, then squeezed Brady's arm. Brady wouldn't admit it, but tears welled up in his eyes at seeing his friend's concern.

Cash huffed a laugh. "Burn the place down, why don't you."

Glad to have the sentimental moment over with, Brady laughed, but started coughing.

Darcie planted her hands on her hips. "All of you back off now. I'll let you know when these two are ready for visitors."

"Yes, ma'am." Cash saluted, and he and Archer went to join Jake.

Darcie might insist he lie on the stupid gurney, but he watched his team hold an impromptu meeting without him. He knew it was futile to try to get up and join them, but honestly, he didn't need to. The frowns traveling around the group told Brady all he needed to know. The fire had been set intentionally and their stalker had upped the ante in his quest to end Morgan's life.

"Dinner," Archer announced to the team gathered in the family room. "It's just burgers, but after the fire, we're lucky we even have a place to cook."

Brady got up, moving slower than his usual agile speed. Morgan watched him step across the family room. He wore gym shorts, his lower leg bandaged. They'd both been evaluated for smoke inhalation and released, so at least that wasn't a problem. But he grimaced as he moved. He was in pain and refused medication in order to remain alert in the event of another attack. She hated to see him suffer, but she appreciated his ongoing sacrifice for her.

"Ready." He held out his hand to help her up.

She took it, and the instant they touched she knew she was facing a losing battle.

He was her hero. Plain and simple. The man who ran through flames to rescue her. The man who kept putting her before himself. How was she going to keep ignoring his fine qualities, ignore the way her heart beat faster around him?

He appraised her. "Everything okay?"

"How's the leg?" she asked quickly to hide her feelings.

"So minor even Darcie can't insist on treating it."

"But I will." The EMT came up behind him and thumped him on the head. She grinned at him as she stepped past them.

Brady's lips turned up in an easygoing smile. He looked boyish and carefree. A look Morgan hadn't seen much of since they'd met. A look that charmed her and made her rush after Darcie so she wouldn't be alone in the room with him.

In the dining room, Brady pulled out a chair and waited for her to be seated, then dropped onto the chair next to her. He was oblivious to her struggle. Probably thinking about his pain or the fire. She wanted to think about anything but the fire. She'd nearly died and the terror still lingered in her heart. Might always linger there.

"Man, you scared us." Cash eyed her as he passed a plate of burgers. "I can't wait to see Skyler's face when she gets back."

"Oh, no, Skyler." Morgan's apprehension rose. "I hadn't even thought about that. I destroyed her condo."

"No." Jake gave a firm shake of his head. "The person who disabled the smoke detectors and torched the place did."

The terrifying ordeal came rushing back. "I can't believe I slept through all of that."

"I can." Darcie frowned. "You've been through a lot. If I had my way, you'd be resting right now."

Archer laughed and looked at Morgan. "It's official. Darcie is mothering you, so you're now a card-carrying member of the group."

Morgan glanced at Brady. He was looking at her, his eyes dark with emotion. She blushed at the implications lingering there and stuffed her burger into her mouth. Her throat was still dry and irritated from the smoke, but even if it wasn't, she'd be hard-pressed to swallow with all eyes on her.

"No need to look so worried, Morgan." Jake's mouth turned up in a rare smile. "We're not a bad group to be affiliated with."

"Oh, I didn't," she said quickly. "I mean, I'm not." She shot a look at Brady. "It's just...I..."

"I'm all for this mushy stuff," Cash teased. "But can we move this along? Krista's waiting for me at her place."

Jake rolled his eyes. "What a difference a year makes."

"I know, right?" Archer said. "We used to be able to count on Cash gagging when things took a turn in this direction but now…"

Cash punched Archer's shoulder. "Time to move on."

Morgan wished she could take his advice and move on. Move on from the fire, from the threats, from these feelings for Brady. She looked at him again and she longed to have someone in her life who wanted to protect and cherish her, to stand beside her and share life's ups and downs. She didn't want to be alone. She really didn't.

Trouble was, she didn't know if she could move on from the huge obstacle that was holding her back from a embracing a relationship with a wonderful man like Brady.

EIGHTEEN

Brady rumbled along the narrow highway in his old pickup truck, a howling wind blowing snow onto the road and slowing his progress. Coming from Minnesota, Brady knew how to drive in the snow, but it snowed so seldom in the Portland area that most drivers didn't have the proper skills.

A fitting end for his night, though. The weather was as miserable as his day had been. He was about ready to call it quits and hope that tomorrow they'd come up with a better lead than Eckert's lock-picking tools. As of now, they were out of ideas. Even the trap set with Morgan's drink bottles hadn't panned out. The FRS team had brainstormed through dinner, trying to think of new avenues to pursue, but came up with nothing new. The stalker had bested them, leaving nothing behind to implicate himself.

But Brady wouldn't give up. Not with the stakes raised. He had to try everything he could, even grasping at straws to find the creep trying to kill

Morgan. In desperation, Brady had moved his attention back to Preston and continued his internet research. He'd discovered Orion Transport had outstanding bills. Lots of them. Enough to put the company in danger of bankruptcy.

Preston needed the merger with Thorsby Mill for an infusion of cash into Orion. Didn't mean he was guilty of anything, but money was a powerful motivator. Which was why Brady was on his way to Orion now. To do what, he didn't know yet. He'd figure that out as he went along.

Nearing Orion's building, he killed his headlights and pulled to the side of the snow-covered road across from the employee parking lot. No way he wanted Preston to know he was spying on him. The old, rundown building was dark except for a few interior lights.

Brady grabbed his night-vision binoculars and other surveillance tools, then quietly slipped through the icy-cold night. He crept close to the property line and lifted his binoculars. A Lexus covered in snow sat in Preston's reserved parking space. An older model sedan with less snow was parked in the next space. Two men dressed in dark colors stood arguing. Brady couldn't hear them but he could see the stiff body language and the way the bigger man fisted his hands.

Brady made his way closer and soon recognized Preston. Brady hadn't a clue about the other man's identity, but he was rugged and as tall as a pine tree. He was dressed in worn jeans and a tattered jacket, obviously not one of Preston's typical associates.

"This is it," Preston said, slapping a wad of cash into the big man's hand. "We're done."

Brady moved even closer. Took out his cell phone and turned on the video recording, hoping the falling snow didn't ruin the video.

The big man stepped toward Preston. "We're done when I say we're done, Hunter. I'm thinking another grand will do it to keep me quiet."

"Please," Preston scoffed. "The last thing you'll do is turn me in. It'll implicate you, too, and you're not going back to jail for breaking and entering."

"See, here's the thing, dude." Big Man pulled a phone from his pocket. "Everything you ever said to me is recorded right here. It's a burner phone, so it won't be traced back to me, but it's enough to send you away for hiring me to break into that chick's place and car to leave your little surprises."

Preston! Preston really is Morgan's stalker.

"Fine," Preston said. "Another grand, but you hand over the phone and that's the end of this."

"Sure," Big Man said. "Get the money and we'll talk."

"Now," Preston growled. "I have the cash in my office. Let's go."

Big Man's mouth fell open. "You have it here?"

Brady heard the panic in Big Man's voice. Most likely, he was hoping to continue to blackmail Preston, but with Preston's quick thinking demanding the phone now, Big Man would have to hand it over.

Hopefully, it would give Brady enough time to get a deputy out here to arrest the two of them. Since they were well outside the city and in County's jurisdiction, Brady could make the arrest himself, but he had a personal stake in this, and he didn't want anything to tarnish the arrest. For that, he'd need an impartial officer. Deputies from his agency patrolled this rural area. Hopefully one of them was available, given the many accidents the snow would bring tonight.

Brady hightailed it back to his vehicle and called it in. Deputy Johnston, an eager young officer who'd joined the staff a year ago, was dispatched. Brady would like a more experienced officer, but Johnston would have to do.

Brady got Johnston on the phone and warned him to arrive without lights and siren. Then he disconnected and kept his binoculars focused on the building in case the men came out. Time ticked by painfully slowly.

"C'mon, c'mon, c'mon," Brady whispered. "Get here already."

He soon heard a car approaching, but as Brady had asked, Johnston had killed his headlights. Brady reached into his truck and flashed his parking lights one time. Johnston eased closer and parked in front of Brady's truck. Brady quickly updated Johnston and handed his binoculars to the tall, gangly deputy so he could peruse the area.

"They're still inside," Brady said. "We'll apprehend them at their cars."

Johnston nodded, and after handing back Brady's binoculars, they moved into position, keeping low so they wouldn't be seen from inside the building. Of course, they'd left a clear trail in the snow, but that couldn't be helped—and if the men stayed inside much longer, fresh snow would cover those tracks. Johnston settled by Preston's car, Brady by Big Man's vehicle. Brady considered changing his mind and taking Preston down himself, but he wouldn't give Preston any reason to use Brady's personal involvement and skate on the charges.

The duo finally came back outside. They were still arguing. Brady allowed the pair to move to their respective cars before drawing his weapon and signaling for Johnston to move out.

"Police," Brady shouted as he charged the cars. "Hands where we can see them."

Preston spun, his feet sliding in the snow. "What's happening?"

Big Man started to bolt, but lost traction and fell. Brady quickly cuffed him.

"C'mon, man, what's going on?" Big Man asked. "What'd we do?"

Brady jerked Big Man to his feet and moved him to join Preston and Johnston.

"You," Preston said after getting a good look at Brady. "What are *you* doing here?"

"Just what it looks like. We're arresting you." Brady let sarcasm flow through his tone.

"For what? This is private property belonging to my family and I'm doing nothing wrong."

Brady dug out his phone and started the video playing.

Emotions raced across Preston's face. Surprise, shock, then that conceited look Brady had come to associate with Preston returned. "You didn't have my permission to record my conversation and it won't stand up in a court of law without other evidence. Which—" he paused and eyed Brady. "I know you don't have."

"True, but it won't be long before we have your partner in crime here—" Brady thumped Big Man's shoulder "—singing like a bird."

Preston eyed the thug. "He won't talk."

"We'll see." Brady read them their rights and made quick work of hauling the pair in to County.

By the time, they'd reached booking, Big Man, aka Eddie Amberg, had agreed to testify against Preston. As the men were processed, Brady called Rossi to inform him of the arrest and invite him to question Preston at County's holding facility, but Brady wasn't going to wait for Rossi to arrive before having a go at questioning Preston.

Brady stepped into the interrogation room and told Preston about Amberg's decision.

"Look," Preston said, sounding bored. "I'm sure we can work something out."

"What did you have in mind?" Brady asked, though it made him nauseous to think about Preston cutting a deal and getting away with nearly killing Morgan.

"I can give you Randall Thorsby, the CEO of Thorsby Mill. He's been dumping bleaching agents into the water for years. And, as a bonus, I can prove he knew all about Morgan being stalked."

Interesting and disgusting. Though Brady really wanted to find out about the stalking, he focused on the dumping first. "If what you say is true, why didn't the water samples at the class-action trial show the bleaching chemicals?"

"Simple. After people started getting sick downriver, Randall cleaned up his act."

"And what about Morgan? Was she in on this?" Brady knew she'd never do something so underhanded, but he had to confirm it for the record.

"Miss Goodie Two-shoes? Are you kidding? No."

"So does the reason you stalked her have something to do with the trial?"

"I didn't admit to stalking her, Owens. You know that. I only mentioned that Randall knew about it. As far as I'm concerned, until my attorney arrives and the DA cuts me a deal in exchange for my information on Randall, I've done nothing wrong." The snarky smile widened.

"Did you poison her to get her come back home and save your company?"

Preston picked a piece of fuzz from his sleeve. "Asked and answered in Portland. Nothing has changed since then."

Brady wanted to wipe the smug look off the guy's face. Instead, he came to his feet and planted his hands on the table. "You may think you're getting away with this, Hunter, but I assure you when you mess with someone I care about—namely Morgan—I will bring the full force of the First Response Squad down on you and that's not something you'll want to have happen."

Preston's smug expression remained fixed in place. Brady dragged in a breath to calm the storm raging inside his body and marched out of the room before he punched Preston and broke the nose that only plastic surgery could have made so perfect.

In the hallway, Brady dug out his phone and dialed Morgan's father. Brady didn't care where Mr. Thorsby was or what he was doing. Brady was going to obtain a confession for the dumping so Preston couldn't use the information to barter a deal. Then Brady could come back here and tell the arrogant Preston Hunter that, with no deal, he was going away for a very long time for stalking.

* * *

Morgan heard a male and female talking in the hallway and her heart rate shot up. After the fire, she didn't feel safe anywhere—not even in Brady's condo, which he'd insisted she use. She ran to the door and looked out the peephole to discover Lacy and Archer. Perfect. Morgan always loved to see Lacy.

She opened the door and smiled at her friend—or should she be saying *friends* now? Was she friends with the FRS members? They seemed to welcome her with open arms, and she'd like to get to know them better. To strike up her friendship with Darcie again.

She turned her smile to Archer and he returned it. He was genteel and reserved, and he reminded Morgan of a more grounded and sincere version of the men she'd grown up around.

"I hope you don't mind having a visitor," he said.

"Mind, are you kidding?" Morgan twined her arm with Lacy's. "I'm glad for the company."

"I'll be downstairs," Archer said. "Let me know if you need anything."

Morgan led Lacy into the condo and closed the door.

Lacy looked around with an odd expression on her face.

"Kind of messy, isn't it?" she said when she noticed Morgan watching her. "Didn't you say Brady was a former Marine? I'd have thought he'd be all neat and organized."

"Messy or not, I'm glad to have a place to stay. Someone started a fire in Skyler's condo. I barely got out in time."

"I know," Lacy said, sounding mad, which Morgan assumed was directed at the arsonist.

"I suppose Archer told you all about it on the way up." Morgan dropped onto the chocolate-brown sofa.

Lacy joined Morgan and started rummaging around in her big leather purse. "I was hoping you'd come back to the office with me."

"Now?"

Lacy looked up from her purse. "I know it's late, but it's about Harold."

"What about him?"

"He just called me. He finally has a second job interview tomorrow and he's feeling uncertain about it. He asked if we would be willing to prep him."

"What time is his interview?"

"First thing in the morning. That's why we have to do it tonight."

"Usually I'd be the first person to help Harold, but I promised Brady I wouldn't go anywhere without him. Besides, you have the skills to do this. You don't really need me."

Lacy's eyes narrowed. "So you're putting yourself first. That's no big surprise."

"What?" Morgan asked as she studied her friend who was rarely negative. "This is the first time I've ever said no."

"Maybe on the job, but…" Lacy ended with a shrug, her expression saying she was itching for a fight.

Morgan had never fought with Lacy, but if she wanted a fight, Morgan had bottled up plenty of frustration over the last few days and she'd be happy to oblige.

"But what?" she challenged, and lifted her chin in defiance while she was at it.

Lacy's eyes darkened, but there was a hint of surprise in them as if she hadn't expected Morgan to defend herself. Lacy frowned and kept digging in her purse until she pulled something out. It took Morgan a few moments to realize Lacy was holding a gun.

"I didn't take you for a gun person," Morgan said, her anger melting when she realized that with all the bad things happening around her, Lacy might be afraid. "But it's okay. You don't need it. The team has upped their vigilance since the fire, and we're safe here."

"Just like you to be so oblivious." Lacy pointed the gun at Morgan.

"What?" Morgan automatically shrank back. "Don't point that at me. It's not funny."

Lacy rolled her eyes. "You really are dense, aren't you? Fine. I'll spell it out. It was me. I'm the one who poisoned you. Who started the fire. And I'm going to kill you. Is that plain enough for you?"

"What? No." Morgan refused to believe what she was hearing. "You're my friend."

"Hardly." Lacy snorted. "You don't know how difficult it was to pretend."

Morgan gaped at Lacy. "Why do it, then?"

"I couldn't poison you if I couldn't get close to you."

Morgan could do nothing but stare at her friend. Lacy, the woman Morgan had bared her soul to for the last few months, when all that time she'd wanted to kill Morgan. Unbelievable.

Sad resignation started setting in. Morgan's already heavy heart overflowed with pain. "I don't understand."

"You never did, did you?" The words were hurled at Morgan. "All those hours in the courtroom. Those of us whose families died, beaten down day after day by your legal maneuverings. People dying each week as you fought to protect your money and play God with our lives."

Morgan searched her memories of the courtroom for Lacy. "You weren't part of the suit. I would recognize your name if you were."

"My parents were registered under my stepfather's last name. But I was there in the back, at the beginning. Until both of my parents got so sick that I had to stay home with them. Care for them.

Watch them suffer and die." Her eyes glazed over for a moment and she waved the gun. "All because of your greed."

"I don't remember seeing you," Morgan said to buy some time to figure a way out of this.

"Of course you don't. You didn't care enough to look at us."

Morgan's anger returned. "That's not true. I saw everyone. Their pain. Their grief. I wanted to help."

"Oh, please. I'm going to kill you no matter what, so don't waste your time and insult me further with that PR speak."

Morgan didn't know what to say. She had seen this same attitude on a daily basis, but between Craig and Lacy, it now hit hard. Morgan knew Lacy. Cared for Lacy. And now, she saw the pain the people suffered even more intimately.

"I'm so sorry for your loss," Morgan said, though she knew it sounded trite and inadequate.

Lacy huffed out a sour laugh. "Right. I could see your sympathy in the courtroom."

"I wish I could have helped."

"No you didn't, or you would have done something."

Lacy was right. Morgan might have seen their pain and wanted to help, but she was too busy worrying about her father and what he might say if they lost the lawsuit to even consider what to do.

Lacy sat up higher and pulled her shoulders

back as if a weight had been lifted from them. "I made it my mission for you to feel our pain. To see what it's like be sick. To feel terrible every day. It would have continued to get worse over time. Until you died. But your stupid boyfriend got in my way, and I had to change course. Start the fire."

"Fire? That was you, too? How did you even know how to break into the condo? Or disable the smoke detectors?"

She laughed. "The internet has everything you could need and more. Amazing what you can learn to do when you're motivated."

"And now you're going to shoot me?"

She simply stared, a stark expression on her face, her chest rising and falling with heavy breaths.

"It doesn't have to be this way," Morgan said in a last ditch effort to save herself. "Even if you kill me, Brady will find you and you'll spend the rest of your life in jail for murder."

"Ha!" Lacy jutted out her chin. "My life is almost over. Thanks to you. To your poison."

Morgan's heart fell. "You have cancer, too?"

"Yes, and I'm not leaving this world alone. I'm taking you with me."

NINETEEN

Eager to question Morgan's father, Brady climbed into his truck. It wouldn't be long. The mill was only five minutes away. Brady settled the keys in the ignition, but let his hand fall. He couldn't go rushing over to Morgan's father without telling her what had happened. She deserved to know about it first. He pressed her icon on his phone. The phone rang, and he sat impatiently waiting to hear her voice again.

Four rings. Five rings. Nothing.

A trickle of apprehension tickled his back. "Don't panic. She could simply be sleeping."

He punched Archer's number.

"Is Morgan okay?" Brady asked the second Archer answered.

"Last I checked, why?"

"She's not answering her phone."

"Maybe she's too busy with Lacy."

"Lacy's there?"

"Yes. Is that a problem?"

"No. I just didn't know she was coming over," Brady said, but something felt wrong. If she was just chatting with her friend, why wouldn't she answer her phone? "Can you go upstairs and tell Morgan I need to talk to her?"

"Sure." Brady heard Archer's feet pounding up the iron steps and then a loud knock sounded on the door.

Brady waited, each second convincing him there was a problem.

"She's not answering," Archer finally said. "Maybe she went somewhere with Lacy."

"She wouldn't do that," Brady snapped out. "At least, I hope she wouldn't."

"Let me look to see if Lacy's car is still here."

Brady's pulse started pounding wildly, and he took a few deep breaths to control the anxiety.

Archer came back on. "Car's gone."

"Then I need you to go into my condo and make sure Morgan's okay."

"I don't have a key."

"Then bust down the door."

"Are you sure?"

"Positive, man, just do it," Brady ground out.

"Okay, but I want to go on record as saying you're off your rocker, and I'm not paying for this door."

"Then I'm off my rocker. Just hurry up and get the door open."

"Fine. I'm putting down the phone for a minute."

Brady listened to loud banging, wood splintering, then Archer called for Morgan. There seemed to be no response to his plea. Brady's gut cramped hard, and he waited for bad news.

"She's not here, man. I'm sorry, I had no idea she'd leave without telling me."

"Or wouldn't answer her phone," Brady said, his minding running over where she could have gone. "Why wouldn't she be answering her cell?"

"Um," Archer said. "It's on the table."

The news felt like a punch to the gut. "Either she forgot it or was compromised and couldn't get to it. Or she could simply be confused from everything that's happened to her."

"Or…" Archer's voice fell off.

"Or what?"

"I've been thinking about the fire and the poisoning. So far, you've been looking for a romantic stalker, right? But neither of these attacks really fit a male stalker's personality."

"How so?"

"Men are more direct. More violent. If they want to hurt someone, they go after them directly with a knife or a gun. Women are usually the ones who want to distance themselves from the act of murder and to keep from personally inflicting physical pain. So they look for less violent ways to kill. Like poison and fire."

Brady appreciated Archer's help, but with Morgan missing, Brady didn't have time to waste. "Cut to the point, man."

"What if the stalking was a set up to throw us off track and you're looking for a woman?"

"A woman?" Brady asked. "Who?"

"I don't know, but if this isn't motivated by romance and this person really wants to make Morgan suffer and die, then I suspect we're actually looking for someone related to the class action trial. Which means we could be looking for a woman."

Brady's panic started growing. "Then I need a list of plaintiffs to see if we recognize a name."

"I have a friend at the clerk's office. She should be able to log in from home and get us what we need."

"Call her, and I'll head over to the mill." Brady explained the situation with Morgan's father. "If your friend can't provide the information, I'll do whatever it takes to get it from Morgan's father."

The wind whipped through trees and blasted snow into Morgan's face, blinding her almost as much as the darkness of night. She was cold, miserable and wet, but Lacy dragged Morgan by the zip ties circling her wrists. They moved through the growing blanket of snow down the familiar path from the mill to the river. As a child, Morgan had run down this path, playing pirates with her cousin. She'd always taken the captain's role, bravely fighting and overcoming the pirates to save her crew and ship. Winning her freedom. Just like she needed to do right now. But this was reality, not playacting.

Morgan could go nowhere in the dark. The only light came from a headlamp Lacy had slipped on at the car. Running away could mean a fall into the icy river.

Lacy picked up speed, the sharp edges of the zip ties sliced into Morgan's skin, which was already raw from rough manhandling. Her legs felt like rubber from fear and sheer exhaustion. Her feet were wet and frozen, but she wouldn't— couldn't—let this take her down. Still, her steps slowed.

"Move," Lacy snapped and jerked hard on a zip tie.

Morgan slipped from the edge of the path into tall scrub. Knee-high grass tangled around her feet as they settled into the heavy snow. She stumbled. Her wrists broke free from Lacy's grasp. Morgan fell hard on her shoulder. Stars danced before her eyes. She recovered quickly and rolled out of the beam of light. Snow slid down her neck, coated her face, but she kept maneuvering until she struggled to her feet. She heard the water to her right so she started to run in the opposite direction, the darkness surrounding her.

Lacy's light slid over the area, back and forth like a searchlight as it glistened on the snow and grew closer. Morgan heard crunching of snow, the light moving more quickly now. Coming even closer. Morgan glanced back just as Lacy launched herself into the air, slamming into Morgan and bringing her down.

"You want to die sooner, I guess," Lacy said with a low growl and pulled a large hunting knife from a sheath on her belt. The bright bream of her headlamp shone in Morgan's eyes. She squinted and saw Lacy bring the knife overhead.

Father, please, oh please, don't let me die.

Lacy pressed the sharp tip against Morgan's throat, piercing delicate skin. Pain sliced through Morgan and brought tears to her eyes, but she wouldn't cry out. She'd do anything not to give Lacy the satisfaction.

Lacy grinned, her face dark and menacing in the shadow of the light. "I'd rather we reached the right spot on the river, but I can do it here if I have to."

"Why here?" Morgan asked trying to buy time.

"You have to ask?" Lacy's voice trembled with excitement. "It's symbolic. The water killed my parents so I'm going to kill you here and dump your body in the water."

"If this was your plan all along, why the stalker thing?"

"First of all, I'm not your stalker."

"You're lying," Morgan said between her teeth.

"Why lie? If I'd done it, trust me, I'd be happy

to admit it." Lacy smiled, her lips flat and grim. "I was perfectly content to watch you get sick from the antifreeze. I didn't need to scare you, too."

Morgan didn't know why Lacy wouldn't admit to the stalking when she'd gladly admit to attempted murder. "This won't bring your parents back, Lacy."

"No, but as I lie on my deathbed, I can remember it. I know how I'm going to go. I've seen it, remember. So in the middle of my pain, when I'm all alone because you killed all of my family, it will give me reason to smile." She grabbed the zip tie and jerked hard. "C'mon. Let's get you secured so I can enjoy every minute of this." She smiled again, her eyes lit by insanity.

She'd been pushed to the edge. No, over the edge. She was truly going to kill Morgan. Right here. Right now. Unless Morgan found a way to save her own life.

Brady wanted to press the gas pedal to the floor, but a snow-covered road would ensure he'd end up in the ditch. He bit his lip and kept his eyes trained ahead to stay on the road. His GPS said Thorsby Mill was a mile down the road, but every moment without knowing where Morgan was or if she was all right seemed like an eternity.

His phone rang from the dash holder. He pulled in a breath. Held it and punched Accept.

"I found it," Archer said, his voice a mixture

of excitement and dread. "A couple died during the trial. Their names are Evangeline and Oliver Fahr. Evangeline is Lacy's mother. Their claim was filed under her stepfather's last name."

"Lacy? Really, Lacy?" Brady nearly lost his dinner. "And you let her into my condo. Do you think—"

"She's taken Morgan somewhere to kill her?" Archer said matter-of-factly when Brady was about to jump out of his skin. "Yeah. That's exactly what I think." Archer fell silent, but Brady heard him moving around in the background.

Brady focused on the dark road ahead as he searched for a way to find Morgan. He came up blank. Nothing. Nada. No way to help the woman he loved.

Loved, really? Yes, really. And he'd do anything to get her back.

"Bingo," Archer shouted. "I know where Morgan is."

Brady's heart soared. "Where? How?"

"I used Morgan's cell to locate Lacy's phone number. It was a long shot, but I asked a buddy at the phone company to ping Lacy's phone before I called you. The coordinates just came back. Morgan's at her family's mill. Specifically, the south side. By the river. I'm texting the coordinates now."

Thank You, God!

"Get backup out here." Brady hung up and cut

off his lights. He swung into the large parking lot, the tires crunching on the fresh snow as his pulse hammered in his head.

Please don't let Lacy see me arrive—and please give me the skills to save Morgan. Please.

Brady jumped from the truck and retrieved his rifle and scope from a locked storage box in truck bed. He pocketed extra ammo and checked his sidearm before shrugging into his ballistic vest. He crept through the scrub as silently as a hunting panther, the snow nothing but an irritant. To become a sniper, he'd had to pass the rigorous stalking portion of the training. The irony of Morgan having a stalker didn't miss Brady, but the stalking he'd trained intensively on was different. He learned to use the terrain, nature, anything around him to disguise his body and not only sneak up to his stand without being seen, but to get off a shot without giving his location away, too.

He was good at it. The best in his class. The best on his sniper team.

Tonight was different. The woman he loved depended on his skills. He had to fight a rush of nerves that put a slight tremble in his hands. Urged him to charge in, maybe making a mistake. He took a deep breath and pushed his emotions to the side, letting his training take over.

He crested the hill on his belly, slowly lifted his night-vision binoculars and swept the area. A light in the distance near a tree caught his eye.

He focused in. Spotted Morgan tied to the thick trunk. He zoomed in on her face. Lacy's head-lamp illuminated Morgan's cold, stark fear as the snow fell softly over her. Despite the cold, Brady's palms started to sweat. Not good for holding his rifle still. For getting a good shot at Lacy.

A knife flashed in the beam of light. Glinting. Sending a warning into the night. Lacy suddenly moved. Started around the tree in long purpose-ful steps. Her body language was jerky and tense, and her mouth was moving rapidly. She was tell-ing Morgan something. Brady wished he could hear her.

Didn't matter, really. She was an immediate threat that needed to be neutralized. But what was the best way? The area was wide open and even with Brady's marked stalking skills, he couldn't get close enough to untie Morgan before Lacy struck. He had no choice. He'd have to shoot.

He looked at Morgan again. He wasn't wor-ried he would hit her, but seeing Lacy fall to the ground from a kill shot right in front of her would devastate her. And he wasn't worried about being able to pull the trigger, either. Not with Morgan in danger. He saved lives. His job was important. Valuable. Not something for people to question or judge him over.

He lowered his binoculars and slowly eased his rifle around. Opened the tripod. Rested it on the hard, packed ground. Sighted Lacy in his scope.

Blew out a breath. Slowed his heart rate—his breathing—and dropped his finger to the trigger.

Morgan struggled against her restraints as Lacy circled, flashing the knife like a sword. Morgan couldn't believe the depth of Lacy's anger. Bitterness had cut her to the core.

Morgan had carried resentment for her father, so she knew how it felt on a much lower level. Her father. She might never see him again. Never be able to make amends. The thought sent a shaft of pain through her heart.

She'd foolishly let her own agenda make things worse between them. If, God forbid, Lacy ended Morgan's life, she'd go to her grave resenting her dad. She couldn't do that.

She closed her eyes and felt each snowflake land on her face. Remembered her joy as a child on the rare occasions when it snowed. Her father letting go and playing with her. Building snowmen. Throwing snowballs.

Where had that man gone? Could she find him again? She had to.

Lord, please forgive me. Forgive Dad. He doesn't know You. Doesn't know how You can change lives. Change him. Let him learn of Your amazing love and change my heart, too. Let me be a witness to him instead of making things worse between us.

If I live, she thought and despite her fear, she

found a small measure of peace and opened her eyes. If she got out of this alive, she'd do her best to make up with her father. To help him find faith. Amazing how seeing the end of her life helped her to accept things she thought were so important and insurmountable.

Including her feelings for Brady. She wished she'd told him how she felt. That he'd become important to her. No, more than important. Necessary.

Give me the chance, Father. Please.

Lacy suddenly stopped her frantic pacing to stand next to Morgan. Eyes that were dark and lifeless locked on Morgan.

Morgan recognized Lacy's grim resolve for what it was. The end. Lacy smiled and raised the knife. The blade caught a shaft of moonlight that broke through the clouds. The snow stopped falling. Morgan's peace fled and terror caught her by the throat. She tried to swallow. To breathe. Couldn't.

A shot rang out. Lacy's hand whipped back. She grabbed her arm and cried out in pain. The knife clattered against a rock and bounced into the dark. She tumbled to the ground. A solid thump sounded, and her lamp extinguished. She didn't make a sound. All was quiet.

A figure in the distance, barreling through the scrub, caught Morgan's attention. The moon shone on him. His body was tall and his steps sure and fluid.

Brady? It had to be. Who else could have gotten off a shot from such a distance and hit a target as small as Lacy's wrist?

Thank You, Father.

"Morgan," he shouted as he approached. "Morgan, call out."

"I'm fine," she yelled back. "You hit Lacy's hand. She dropped the gun. She's on the ground. Not moving."

He bounded into the clearing. Dropped to his knees.

Morgan couldn't see him, but she heard him moving around and then the metallic sound of handcuffs clicking into place. Her knees felt weak at the blessed, wonderful sound.

Brady came to his feet. "Lacy's alive. She hit a rock and has a head wound." He stood and moved toward Morgan. "Local authorities are on the way. Let me get those restraints off."

She couldn't wait for him to free her so she could throw her arms around his neck and hold him close. "How did you find me?"

"I was on the way to talk to your dad and called you. Found out you were missing. Archer suggested that fire and poison were often methods women used to kill so he reviewed the plaintiff list to look for a woman and found Lacy's connection. Then he found her phone number in your cell and tracked her GPS."

The ropes fell off as sirens sounded in the distance. Brady sliced through the zip ties, the muscles in her arms feeling as if they were tearing as she pulled them forward.

He came around front. Cupped her face. "Are you really okay, honey?"

"I am now that you're here." She smiled. "I'll always be good with you nearby."

His eyes locked on hers. Searched, probed. His gaze heated up, blazing with warmth. He lowered his head and his lips descended on hers. Warm, giving, he kissed her gently. Softly. She was aware of raised voices heading toward them, but she couldn't move. Didn't even try to move. It was high time she accepted the fact that when it came to Brady she was powerless to resist.

TWENTY

Morgan sat in the passenger seat of Brady's truck, waiting for him to say goodbye to whoever he was talking with on the phone. The call had come in a few moments ago, and he'd looked so serious before stepping away. She'd known it was important and he had to take it, but she hated being separated from him for even these few moments. As if he felt her eyes on him, he turned and met her gaze. She smiled. He returned it with an intimate smile that melted her heart.

He hastily said something, then jogged to the truck and slid in. "There's something I have to tell you that you're not going to like."

"What? You're married," she joked, because she didn't think she could handle one more bit of bad news today and his serious tone said it was going to be very bad news.

He didn't return her smile, raising her apprehension even more.

"What is it?" she whispered.

"Your father," he said not looking away. "Preston claims your father knowingly discharged bleaching chemicals into the river."

"No!" Morgan jerked back and shook her head hard. "No. Dad may not be the nicest of men, but he wouldn't do something like that. Preston must be lying."

Brady reached for her hand again, and she tucked it under her leg. She could see that she'd hurt him, but she couldn't accept comfort when she was still reeling from the news that her father allowed dangerous chemicals to contaminate water used by thousands of people. That he was the reason so many people died and their families suffered.

"Here's the thing," Brady continued. "Before I knew you were missing, I overheard Preston talking to a man he paid to leave the roses and pictures for you while Preston was out of town. Orion Transport's in financial trouble, and he was trying to scare you into moving home where he could get back together with you and merge the companies to save Orion."

Morgan tightened her fingers into a fist. "You must be wrong. He's engaged to Natasha."

Brady took a deep breath and Morgan dreaded the next words from his mouth. "That was Jake on the phone. Preston admitted he wasn't engaged when he first started taking the pictures of you. When Natasha came into his life, he saw an easier way to get his hands on money. Problem was, her family had financial issues, too, and she was planning to marry Preston for *his* money. When Preston discovered that, he returned to scaring you, but stayed with Natasha to throw you off track."

Brady paused and Morgan knew more bad news was coming. "Preston provided proof that your father knew about the stalking, too."

"No," she said, but the word held no weight. "It can't be true."

"I'm sorry, honey, but it is. The DA has already reviewed the evidence and offered Preston immunity for the stalking."

"Why would the DA agree to that?"

"Preston's going to testify against your father. This is an election year and the DA wants a big win that will touch the voters' hearts."

"No," she said again, but it was nothing more than a whisper. She bit her lip, thinking, and her plea to God not even an hour ago came back. She'd begged Him to allow her to let go of the resentment toward her father. To let her father know Him.

"I need to talk to my dad," she said, and hoped God would give her the right words to say.

Brady kept his gaze glued on her. "That's not a good idea, honey."

"I've got to face him, or I won't be able to move on."

"Fine," Brady agreed reluctantly. "But you can't tell him anything about Preston."

"I can do that." She clutched Brady's arm. "Can we go see him now? I want this all done with and behind me."

"I was supposed to meet with him so I know he's in his office." Brady sat silently for a long moment, then leaned forward and kissed her forehead. "I'll be right by your side when you talk to him. I'm there if you need me, okay?" He gave a lopsided grin that melted her heart.

"Absolutely."

He fired up the pickup and they drove to the far side of the building where her father's office was located. Thankfully, it was far enough from where Lacy had dragged her that he wouldn't have seen or heard the commotion. He met them at the door and invited them up to his office. He offered Brady a scotch, but ignored Morgan. Right. Just as expected. He didn't think she could do anything for him, so why waste his efforts on social niceties?

Brady declined the drink, stepped closer to Morgan and took her hand.

She smiled up at him, squeezed his hand, then freed herself and approached her father's desk.

"You lied to me," she said, making sure to keep all hurt from her voice and stick to the facts. "Not only were bleaching agents discharged into the river, but you knew all about it and covered it up so you wouldn't have to take responsibility for the lives you ruined."

He dropped into his desk chair and jutted out his chin. "Says who?"

"I'm not at liberty to say."

"But you believe this allegation against me?"

Confronting him was a lot harder than she'd expected and emotions surged through her body. She felt like she was a little girl, standing before his big desk, asking for something she knew he'd deny. She didn't trust her voice so she nodded. Brady must have picked up on her unease as he stepped up next to her.

Her father's lips narrowed in a tight smile. "Doesn't matter, now, does it? There's no proof."

Her mouth dropped open for a moment. "So you're saying you did it?"

He smirked. "Not saying I did. Just saying *if* I did something like that, I'd make sure there wasn't any proof."

Morgan knew her father. This was not only a confession, but he was bragging about how he would hide it. He was nothing like the fine, honorable and forthright man standing beside her who would help her deal with yet another blow to her life.

The urge to yell at her father, to chastise him for hurting people, was strong, but she remembered her prayer and took a second to compose herself. "Things will go easier for you if you confess, Dad.

I'll even help work on your defense and get you the best deal possible."

He shot to his feet, his eyes dark with anger. "I'm not worried, little lady. They won't be able to prove anything."

Brady glared at her father. "You're wrong, Mr. Thorsby. We have all the proof we need. You're going down for this, and despite the way you've treated Morgan over the years, she's trying to help you. Open your eyes and see her. She's an amazing woman who could teach you so many things."

Her father arched a brow. "If she wanted to help me, she would never have left the company."

Morgan's heart ached for the pain she heard in his voice. "I had to leave, Dad. Before I became as jaded and cynical as you are. Life isn't all about money or things it can buy. It's about so much more, and I want to help you see that."

He took a step back and, for the first time in her life, she saw him hesitate. This was a start. A good start. Hopefully, she'd put a chink in his impenetrable armor, and if she backed off now maybe he'd see the right thing to do and turn himself in. He'd be facing a long prison term, but she'd visit him and share her faith. And, God willing, her father would finally discover the real meaning of life.

Brady hugged Morgan to his side as they walked to his truck. She was trembling. He didn't know if it was anger at her father's treatment or the pain of fully seeing him for who he really was. It had hurt her, badly, and Brady didn't know what to do about it except help her into the pickup.

He took the driver's seat and swung the truck onto the highway so he could get her as far from the mill as possible. "I'm sorry, honey. About your dad, I mean."

She sighed. "You know, I thought I'd put all this behind me when I moved out of the guesthouse, but I guess I haven't."

"It's not an easy thing to do."

She swiveled to face him. "You sound like you speak from experience."

His first response was to shut down as he always did, but if he was going to have a meaningful relationship with Morgan, he had to tell her about his past. "Actually, we have a lot in common here."

"Did your father treat you like this, too?"

"Father? No. I don't even know who my father is, and my childhood was just the opposite of yours, but it left similar scars."

She shifted closer. "Tell me about it."

"My mother's an alcoholic," he started before he chickened out. "We didn't have money like you. I grew up in a ratty old trailer park. Other kids teased me, and I felt like trash. Mom managed to keep her problem under control most of the time and hold down a job, but everyone in our small town knew her problem. Honestly, I resented her until yesterday and let it eat at me."

She took his hand resting on his knee. "Yesterday?"

He wasn't used to spilling his guts, and he felt as exposed as the kid in hand-me-downs standing in front of a school assembly to receive an FHA award for Bessie. He curled his fingers around the wheel and squeezed. "See, here's the thing. While you were in the hospital, I had a lot of time to think about how you were poisoned. Somehow, I went from thinking about physical poison to emotional poison." He paused and glanced at her to gauge her interest.

"Go on," she encouraged.

"I listened to their opinions of me. Of my mom. And let them define who I was. I've always felt lacking. Like I wasn't good enough. Everywhere but in the marines. But you know what?" he asked, eager to share his recent revelation. "Holding on to stuff like that doesn't work. It's like taking poison and expecting the people who hurt you to die. But they don't. They go on with life as if nothing happened. They may not even remember the hurt they inflicted—"

"While you're hurting inside," she finished for him. "That's profound, Brady."

"Yeah, kind of deep for me, right?" He grinned.

"Don't." She tightened her grip. "Don't joke about it like you always do. You're an amazing man. One I'm proud to know. Proud to call my friend. Money means nothing to you, which is exactly the way it should be. You're twice the man my father and Preston are, and your insight could very well give me the help I need to let go of this latest news about my father."

"That's good, then," Brady said, and stared at the road ahead.

It had felt good to open up. To see she didn't care about his past, about his lack of money. It meant he could pursue her and not worry about his financial status. But she'd called him friend. Just friend. Even after the kiss they'd shared, she said friend.

He looked at her, but she was staring off into the distance. She'd been through so much and it wasn't the time to press her. He'd settle for friend. For now, but that was going to change as soon as the opportunity presented itself.

After answering all the questions and giving her statement, Morgan was beat and didn't want to socialize with the FRS members. At the firehouse door, she hung back and admired the strings of Christmas lights reflecting like stars in the snow. She'd forgotten Skyler was due to return tonight for the special Christmas party she hosted for her team members.

Morgan suspected everyone would be dressed up, and she was covered with mud and grime from

Lacy's attack. So was Brady, but it didn't seem to faze him. He escorted her into the family room where the entire team and their significant others had gathered, and as she suspected, they were wearing dressy attire. The Christmas tree was lit, as were the zillion candles in the room along with lights twinkling on the fireplace and the banister.

The place felt so welcoming. So warm and peaceful, but Morgan didn't know what her role was with the FRS team. Her role with Brady was equally confusing. After nearly dying and the kiss they'd shared, she was certain of her feelings for him. She wasn't certain of what it meant for her future, though. It had made sense for her to be here when she was in danger, but now...what was her purpose here?

Darcie caught sight of Morgan and rushed across the room, her high heels clipping loudly across the concrete floor. She lifted Morgan's chin and eyed her carefully. "You weren't hurt?"

Morgan laughed. "Relax, I'm fine. I've already been checked over by the medic called to the scene if you don't believe me."

Darcie frowned. "No one is as thorough as I am."

"Isn't that the truth?" Brady grinned. "Sometimes painfully true."

Darcie rolled her eyes. "Hey, I've saved your hide a time or two, so I wouldn't complain."

He gave Darcie a quick hug, his eyes alive with

something Morgan hadn't seen in him before. A petite woman wearing a sparkling red dress, her hand outstretched, came around to them.

"I'm Skyler," she said, taking Morgan's hand. "Everyone's been filling me in on what I've missed. I'm sorry you went through so much, but I would've loved to have been in on that investigation."

Morgan opened her mouth to apologize for destroying the condo, but a tall, handsome man in a black suit stepped up and rested his hands on Skyler's shoulders.

"My wife—I love how that sounds, by the way—" he paused to grin down at her "—loves nothing more than a challenging investigation when she's not negotiating some standoff and is wearing her deputy's Special Investigator hat."

"Ah, no, husband." She smiled up at him. "I love you more."

"Well, that's a given." He drew her under his arm.

Darcie made a fake gagging sound.

"I second that," Archer added.

"Now, come on, guys," Krista said. "Nothing to gag about there. I mean, I can totally relate." She pointed at the mistletoe above her head and kissed Cash soundly. The group groaned.

Cash broke free. "You're ruining my reputation here, sweetheart."

"Yeah, Krista. No playing kissy-face with the

big tough guy," Brady joked, but at the same time he slipped his hand over Morgan's and gave her a long, lingering look.

"Great." Darcie eyed them. "Another one bites the dust."

"What are you talking about?" Jake asked.

"Love is in the air." Darcie held up their entwined hands. "These two."

Blushing, Morgan shot a quick look at Brady. His eyes were filled with a mixture of happiness and uncertainty.

Did he love her? Would he want a life with her? If so, could she give up her independence?

Memories of their time together came flashing back. For the most part, he'd never pushed her into making a decision or tried to control her, but had been sensitive. Picked up on how she was feeling and let her express her emotions, then gave her space to work things out.

With a guy like Brady in her life, she didn't have to give up her independence. If she doubted it, she could just look at the men and women in this room. They each stood on their own. Strong and confident, yet they relied on each other all the time.

And who did she have? Who could she rely on?

No one. Her heart ached with the thought. She needed someone in her life. Wanted someone in her life.

Not just someone. Brady. And it was about time she told him that.

Dinner passed slowly. Plates clanked and voices were raised and happy over Morgan's safety and this time to celebrate the birth of Jesus together in their magnificent home. A home that would be Morgan's, too, if Brady had anything to say about it. He could hardly sit still for wanting to talk to her. Sure, fine, being antsy was in his nature, but he had a good reason tonight. He'd waited for Morgan to process the earlier incidents, but he could stand it no longer. He had to tell her how he felt.

He jumped to his feet, grabbed her hand and tugged her up. "If you'll excuse us, I need to talk to Morgan."

"You can talk to her right here," Darcie joked.

"Alone." The word came out more forcefully than he'd intended and Morgan frowned. "Don't worry," he said, "this isn't more bad news." At least he hoped she didn't see it as bad news.

He led her through the family room, grabbed their jackets, then escorted her outside. The night was now clear as a bell. A bright moon illuminated the garden and stars twinkled overhead. A tall Christmas tree strung with colorful lights bathed the area in vivid colors, and the fresh blanket of snow on the ground felt like a new beginning. The beginning he craved.

"What is it?" Morgan asked, bringing his attention back to her.

"I'm not real good about beating around the bush so I'll just come out and say it." He ran his fingers over her cheek. "This thing between us. It's more than a thing. I love you, Morgan."

She smiled up at him. "How long have you been waiting to say that?"

"I've known I have feelings for you for days, but when you were missing? My feelings hit me like a ton of bricks."

"I was a bit slower. I just figured it out when we got here."

"You feel the same way, then?" he asked, needing to hear the words.

"Yes, Brady. I love you." She twined her fingers with his. "Why did you wait to tell me?"

"I wanted this to be special. Not with cops swarming around us and a woman in handcuffs next to us. But in a place like this. Under the stars."

"Why Brady Owens, you're a romantic at heart."

"I guess I am," he said, and felt his face flush.

"That's nothing to be embarrassed about." She freed her hand and rested both of them on his broad shoulders. "In fact, it's something I find quite wonderful, and I'm sure will find even more wonderful in years to come.

He pulled her close, kissed her soundly, then

kissed her again. Longer. Deeper. Losing track of all time and place. This was perfect. She was perfect for him.

Catcalls coming from inside finally broke through. He turned to the family room window where his teammates stood, cheering and whistling.

"Sorry about that," he said. "There's no real privacy around here."

"I'd have it no other way," she said with a mischievous grin. "That is, until we get married and we're on our honeymoon. Then if I discover an FRS member within fifty feet—no make that a mile of us—I'll be gunning for bear."

"Don't worry, honey." Brady drew her against him and held her tightly. "I'll take care of the shooting in this family. A mile is a challenge, but I'm sure if it means being alone with you, I'll make a record shot." He chuckled and felt her laughing against his chest.

As he gazed over her head at the star lighting the top of the tree, the words "peace on Earth and goodwill toward men" took on a new meaning for him. For the first time in his life, he felt a contentment that transcended all understanding, and he knew by Morgan's contented sigh that she felt the same peace, too.

* * * * *

Dear Reader,

As we conclude the third book in the First Responders series, I hope my series theme of finding peace in trying times is coming through. Many people seek to find peace or comfort in the things they own or the money they have. But what do you own that gives you peace? Nothing. Not even money, as it all can be taken in a flash. No one can take away the peace found by trusting in God's provisions and it's truly the only peace found on this Earth.

If you'd like to learn more about this new series, stop by my website at www.susansleeman.com. I also love hearing from readers so please contact me via email, susan@susansleeman.com, on my Facebook page, www.facebook.com/SusanSleemanBooks, or write to me at Love Inspired, 233 Broadway, Suite 1001, New York, NY 10279.

Susan Sleeman

LARGER-PRINT BOOKS!

GET 2 FREE LARGER-PRINT NOVELS PLUS 2 FREE MYSTERY GIFTS

Love Inspired®

Larger-print novels are now available...

LILP15

YES! Please send me **The Montana Mavericks Collection** in Larger Print. This collection begins with 3 FREE books and 2 FREE gifts (gifts valued at approx. $20.00 retail) in the first shipment, along with the other first 4 books from the collection! If I do not cancel, I will receive 8 monthly shipments until I have the entire 51-book Montana Mavericks collection. I will receive 2 or 3 FREE books in each shipment and I will pay just $4.99 US/ $5.89 CDN for each of the other four books in each shipment, plus $2.99 for shipping and handling per shipment.*If I decide to keep the entire collection, I'll have paid for only 32 books, because 19 books are FREE! I understand that accepting the 3 free books and gifts places me under no obligation to buy anything. I can always return a shipment and cancel at any time. My free books and gifts are mine to keep no matter what I decide.

263 HCN 2404 463 HCN 2404

Name	(PLEASE PRINT)

Address	Apt. #

City	State/Prov.	Zip/Postal Code

Signature (if under 18, a parent or guardian must sign)

Mail to the **Reader Service**:
IN U.S.A.: P.O. Box 1867, Buffalo, NY 14240-1867
IN CANADA: P.O. Box 609, Fort Erie, Ontario L2A 5X3